CHRISTOPHER AND THE CLOCKMAKERS

Also by Sara Ware Bassett

THE YOUNG ENGINEERS

Carl and the Cotton Gin
Christopher and the
    Clockmakers
Paul and the Printing Press
Steve and the Steam Engine
Ted and the Telephone
Walter and the Wireless

THE STORY OF

The Story of Glass
The Story of Leather
The Story of Silk
The Story of Sugar
The Story of Porcelain
The Story of Lumber
The Story of Wool

This edition published 2026
by Living Book Press
Copyright © Living Book Press, 2026

ISBN: 978-1-76153-517-8 (hardcover)
           978-1-76153-532-1 (softcover)

First published in 1925.

This edition is based on the 1925 printing by Little, Brown, and Company.

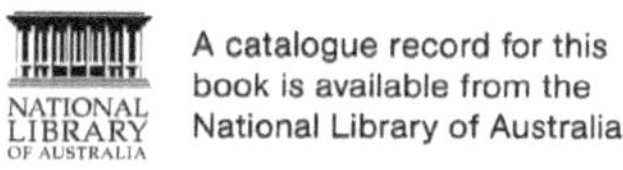

A catalogue record for this book is available from the National Library of Australia

CHRISTOPHER AND THE CLOCKMAKERS

by

SARA WARE BASSETT

"THOSE MEN—ONE OF THEM TOOK A RING—I SAW HIM."

Contents

1. A CLOUD WITH A SILVER LINING — 1
2. CHRISTOPHER MAKES AN ACQUAINTANCE — 10
3. CHRISTOPHER ESCAPES BEING A HERO — 27
4. AN ENCOUNTER WITH THE POLICE — 34
5. CHRISTOPHER ASTONISHES HIMSELF — 42
6. CLOCKS THAT WERE GOOD AS PLAYS — 55
7. AN EXCURSION — 70
8. AN ADVENTURE — 87
9. CHRISTOPHER RECOGNIZES AN OLD ACQUAINTANCE — 97
10. AN AMAZING ADVENTURE — 108
11. THE SEQUEL TO THE LETTER — 118
12. CLOCK GIANTS — 127
13. CLOCKS ON LAND AND CLOCKS AT SEA — 139
14. HOW RUBIES, SAPPHIRES, AND GARNETS HELPED TO TELL TIME — 151
15. CLOCKS IN AMERICA — 160
16. WHAT MASSACHUSETTS CONTRIBUTED — 172
17. THE ROMANCE OF THE WATCH — 185
18. CHRISTOPHER HAS A BIRTHDAY — 201

CHAPTER I

A CLOUD WITH A SILVER LINING

CHRISTOPHER MARK ANTONY BURTON was a tremendously imposing name to give a baby. When he lay in his crib, wee and helpless, he looked as if he might never survive the weight of it. Even later, when he began to toddle about on his small, unsteady feet, the sonorous pseudonym trailed in his wake, threatening to drag him down to an early grave.

Nevertheless his father protested against the burden being lightened one iota. Christopher Mark Antony Burton he had been christened and Christopher Mark Antony Burton he must remain. Had it not been his father's, his grandfather's, and his great-grandfather's name before him; and all his life had not Mr. Burton longed for some one to whom to pass on the treasure of which he was so proud? And then on a happy day a son came upon the scene and *presto*, before the boy was an hour old, the ponderous appellation was clapped on his unlucky head.

Mr. Burton, however, did not consider the child unlucky—not he! To bestow this signal honor afforded him infinite satisfaction. No gift he could have granted his heir could, in his opinion, equal—much less surpass—this one.

He had, to be sure, on the day of the baby's birth, deposited in the savings bank five hundred dollars to its credit; but what was money when weighed against being Christopher Mark Antony Burton, the fourth?

And Christopher had thrived despite the fact that life, no respecter of persons, did not spare him the misfortunes common to the race. He had whooping cough, measles, and mumps like other children, and when at length he reached the ripened age of six he was led to school and it was here, with one swift, leveling blow, that his splendor vanished even as the grass which in the morning groweth up and at night is cut down, and withereth.

He issued forth from his home as Christopher Mark Antony Burton and returned to it shorn of his glories and as plain Chris Burton. Was ever transformation more complete? Certainly not in the estimation of his father and mother. But Chris himself was overjoyed at the emancipation. It seemed as if a ball had been lifted from his foot and left him free as air. And the wonderful part of it was that the operation had been so quickly and painlessly accomplished. It had taken a round-faced, red-haired urchin just about fifteen seconds to sever his bonds.

"Christopher Mark Antony Burton!" jibed he with sardonic glee. "Haw, haw! Can you beat it? Cut it out, Chris."

Whereupon a group of derisive youngsters had proceeded without further ado to cut it out.

"Chris Burton! Chris Burton!" they piped, capering gleefully about their victim.

Christopher's consent to this re-christening was not asked. The name would have been cut in the same ruthless fashion whether he willed it or not. Fortunately, however, he welcomed his release, and this cheerful conformity to public sentiment earned for him at the outset of his career vast popularity.

"Chris is all right," conceded his judges. "Poor kid! Is it his fault if they pasted a mile-long label on him?"

Indeed common opinion generally agreed that the unhappy victim of the Burton honors was far more sinned against than sinning, and his cause was forthwith taken up with zealous sympathy.

"They didn't do a thing to you, you poor trout, when they wished that tag on you, did they?" Billie Earnshaw, the leader of the gang, declared not unkindly. "No matter, old chap! Cheer up! Forget it! We're going to."

And they did. As completely as if the awful appellation had never existed it was wiped from the tablets of their memory and Christopher Mark Antony Burton fourth became Chris Burton—nothing more.

Oh, there were days when the original horror bobbed up. It appeared on report cards and in school registers traced in the teacher's clear, painstaking hand: *Christopher Mark Antony Burton*; nevertheless she never troubled to address him in that fashion. Perhaps she hadn't the time. Life was a busy enterprise and the days were short. One could not stop to roll out a name like that unless blessed with leisure. Accordingly in the school-room our hero passed as Burton and on the ball-field as Chris, and since his existence alternated 'twixt these two worlds, he was Christopher Mark Antony Burton only at breakfast and at bed-time—intervals so brief that they were endured with cheerfulness and complacency.

Therefore having rid himself thus early in his career of a stigma that threatened to blast his chance for success, the future stretched before him smooth as a macadam road. Uneventfully he finished the grammar school and went on into the high school as did other boys of his acquaintance. He was not, however, a scholar who leaped avidly toward books. Painfully, reluctantly he trudged his way. Learning came hard—especially Latin,

French, and history. To hold fast a French verb was for him a thousand times harder than to grip in his clutch a writhing eel; and as for algebra—well, the unknown quantity was the only one he was sure of.

Yet notwithstanding his scholastic limitations, he contrived to wriggle along until at the beginning of his junior year he was whisked away to the hospital with scarlet fever, after which, amid sage waggings of their heads, a group of doctors congregated about his bed. He was not to be alarmed, they said. His eyes were not permanently injured. Yet there was no denying his illness had seriously weakened them and they must be given a long vacation. Perhaps six months might do what was necessary—perhaps, on the other hand, it might take a year. Rest was the thing needed—absolute rest and protection from the light. Whereupon, having delivered themselves of this decree, they placed upon his nose a pair of blue goggles, told him to cheer up, and went their way.

At first the tragedy on which they commiserated him did not appear to Christopher very great. He detested books. Now, without effort of his own, he was to be released from them. It was almost too good to be true. Had he begged the boon on bended knees, his parents would have denied it. And now, as if by magic, the favor he sought had been granted without so much as a word from them. The law had been laid down so forcefully that neither they nor he dared disobey it.

In fact it was soon apparent they felt vastly sorry on Christopher's account that the mandate had been pronounced. Everybody did. Ill news travels as if on wings, and before the boy had been home a day the entire community was offering him sympathy for a calamity which did not seem to him any calamity at all.

True, he detested his blue glasses and would gladly have consigned them to the ash barrel. Still no sky is without shadows; one must take the cake as well as the frosting. Certainly he found it no cross to rise in leisurely fashion while the other kids were hiking along to school and sit down to a hot breakfast cooked especially for him; nor, when the bells were just about ringing for recitations, could it be considered a hardship to saunter off for a tramp in the sunshine, with Joffre, his tireless collie, bounding on before him.

No, his lot was far from an unhappy one. For a week or two he was entirely content. Of course there was no denying there were moments that dragged. He couldn't read, and he had always derived keen delight from a good pirate story. However, people read to him, and that was the next best thing. Often his father or his mother would toss aside their books or papers and read aloud to him an entire evening. But the books they selected were never pirate stories. Instead they were almost always things that aimed to improve him, and if there was anything Christopher resented, it was being improved. Therefore while he appreciated the good intentions of his parents in reading and explaining to him Emerson's essays, he would as lief have exchanged all of them for a single chapter of "Treasure Island." But, alas, his father was not of the "Treasure Island" sort, and neither was his mother. Indeed it is doubtful whether they would have recognized Silver had they met him in broad daylight, on the main street. As for himself he missed Silver sadly—Silver, Deerslayer, and all the rest of his cronies, and before long time began to hang heavily on his hands.

Elversham was, it is true, a beautiful suburb in which to live. Still, there wasn't much doing in it. If your day was not filled with school, baseball, football, or building a radio, how was a chap to fill up his time? He could, of course, go down to the athletic field and watch the games, but as he was accustomed to being in the thick of them, he derived no great pleasure from sitting about on the edges and looking on, while others fumbled the ball or failed to make a touchdown. What a pity it was that when he had dropped out of school he had been obliged to sacrifice his position on the team! Still how could any one be mixed up in a football tackle if he had to wear blue glasses every minute?

No, for the present he must certainly keep out of athletics. He was, in fact, pretty well out of everything. When he joined the fellows, it was only to hear them joshing about some event wholly unintelligible to him. All their jokes and horse play led back to the classroom until at length he felt as if he might as well have listened to a lot of jibbering Chinese as to try to understand their nonsense.

Yes, he was out of it—completely out of it! Gradually the realization dawned on him. He was out of everything, the only idle person in a rushing world. When he took a walk, except for the companionship of Joffre, he went alone. Everybody was too busy to pay any attention to him. He was bored with his own society—horribly bored.

"Isn't there anything I can do, Dad?" he desperately inquired one evening, after his mother had all but read him to sleep with the life of Benjamin Franklin.

"What do you mean, son?" asked Mr. Burton, dropping his paper and emerging abruptly from Wall Street, his attention arrested more by the lad's tone than by his words.

"I mean isn't there anything at all I can do? I'm sick to death of loafing round this house."

"But I thought you were rather pleased to be out of school," Mr. Burton asserted with surprise.

"I was at first—pleased as Punch; but I'm not now. I'm bored within an inch of my life. I can't keep tramping round with Joffre from morning to night, nor is there anywhere to go if I could. Besides, I haven't a soul to speak to—everybody is studying or else playing football."

"It is hard, Christopher," agreed his mother with instant sympathy. "You have been very patient."

"So you have, my boy! So you have!" Mr. Burton echoed. "I had no idea, however, that you were unhappy. Well, well! We must see what can be done."

He rose and began to pace the floor thoughtfully.

"Now if I could afford it," he went on, "I should pack you off on a trip round the world. That would not only amuse you royally but afford you a liberal education into the bargain; but I haven't the money to do that just now, I'm afraid. Some more modest entertainment must be found. H-m! I don't suppose as a makeshift you would care to go into the store with me for a week or two until a better plan can be devised."

The lad's face instantly brightened.

"Yes, I would," he cried. "I'd like it very much." Although the scheme was not a brilliant one, it was far better than hanging about Elversham day after day. To go to the city would mean new sights, new sounds, and doubtless luncheon with his father—a treat to which he had always looked forward since a small boy.

"Really now!" commented Mr. Burton, beaming down at him. "Well, I am surprised. I feared you would not even listen to the proposal. So you like it, eh? Oh, not for long, of course—I understand that; but simply as a filler."

Christopher was all cordiality.

"It wouldn't be half bad."

"Don't imagine I shall set you to work," continued Mr. Burton hastily.

"I'd rather work if there was anything I could do."

"I am afraid there wouldn't be," was the reply. "Ours is a trade that has, for the most part, to be learned."

"I suppose so."

"No, I shall not set you to work—or entertain you, either. You will have to look out for yourself. However, as you say, it may amuse you to go to the store, and perhaps when you get there you can make some sort of a niche for yourself. We'll see."

"Certainly there must be errands to run," Christopher suggested.

Mr. Burton eyed the boy pleasantly, but shook his head.

"Even our errands have to be detailed to skilled men—at least, most of them. Now and then, it is true, there are ordinary messages to be delivered; but in most cases any packages we send out are too valuable to be entrusted to boys your age. They might be held up."

"Held up!" repeated Christopher incredulously.

"Surely. Such things have happened," Mr. Burton nodded. "We never feel safe about sending out valuable goods unless they are well guarded."

"It would be mighty exciting to be held up!" Christopher gasped, his eyes wide with interest.

"Exciting!" mimicked his father sarcastically. "Exciting! Humph! I guess you would find it something more than exciting if a group of yeggs thrust a pistol under your nose. You seem to forget that persons who hold up a messenger do it to get the goods."

"But they don't always succeed?" came breathlessly from Christopher.

"Not in moving pictures," was the grim retort. "In the movies, somebody always happens along at the crucial moment, rescues the hero, captures the villain, and everything is all right. That is the sort of hold-up you are accustomed to, son. But in real life the villain is a desperate character armed with a gun that goes off. You forget that."

Christopher looked crestfallen and flushed uncomfortably.

"Perhaps I am shaking your courage a little and you won't be so eager to go to town with me," jested Mr. Burton.

"On the contrary, the scheme appeals to me more than ever."

"You actually hanker to meet a bandit or two?"

"It would certainly add a thrill to life to encounter a bandit," grinned Christopher.

"Add a thrill!" Mr. Button sniffed. "Add a thrill! Well, I will tell you right now that when you feel a desire for a thrill like that coming on, you can go straight to the movies and indulge it. You shall have no such thrills at *my* expense," and without more ado Christopher Mark Antony Burton, senior, lighted a fresh cigar, took up his paper, and dismissed the matter.

CHAPTER II

CHRISTOPHER MAKES AN ACQUAINTANCE

THE jewelry house of Burton and Norcross occupied four stories of a corner fronting two busy city streets and before its gem-filled windows a group of passers-by were continually standing.

On cushions of velvet lay an alluring display of rings, broaches, necklaces, and costly frivolities of every description while on other cushions ticked watches varying from toy affairs on ribbons to more serious-intentioned and dignified repeaters.

All day and indeed all night, for that matter, a white light beat down upon this flashing outlay, and before it envious spectators flattened their noses against the massive plate glass and dreamed idle dreams of possession.

"Say, Jim, ain't that red stone with the diamonds round it a peach? Gee, but I'd like a thing like that on my finger! How much do you s'pose you'd have to pay for it?"

"A cool hundred, likely."

"Go on!"

"Sure you would. Them red stones are rubies and they cost like the dickens. I ain't sure you wouldn't have to pay mor'n a hundred for that ring."

"Humph! I see myself doin' it!"

"So do I!"

"Well, you needn't rub it in. Anyhow, even if I had the price, I'd rather spend it on a Ford."

"What's the matter with havin' 'em both? You're full as likely to have one as the other; come on. What's the good of standin' here lettin' your mouth water over things there's no hope of your gettin'? Let's call it off an' go to a picture show."

A moment later another pair would saunter up and stop.

"Oh, Mame, look at that diamond necklace! Isn't it wonderful! Do you s'pose it's real?"

"Real! You bet your life it's real! You won't catch Burton and Norcross putting fake diamonds in their window. Come along, for heaven's sake; I'm starving and want my lunch. It's no use to hang round here staring in."

"I can look, can't I?"

"If you want to, yes. Lookin's a cheap entertainment. You're silly to do it though. It'll only get you out of sorts."

So babbled the crowd.

A listener might have amused himself the whole day long enjoying the comments of the throng had he nothing better to do than loiter near by. Unfortunately, however, the corner did not foster extended loitering. It was far too busy a spot. About it swirled and surged an eddy of shoppers, all hurrying this way and that and jostling one another so mercilessly that he who did not make one of the current and move with the stream was all but exterminated. Like a tidal wave, the ruthless concourse swept past, bearing with it everything that obstructed its path. You went whether you would or no, and afterward you stepped into a doorway, caught your breath, straightened your hat, and tried to remember what it was you had intended to do.

By contrast the interior of Burton and Norcross was painfully still. The moment a visitor crossed its threshold he realized that. As if he had left behind him a stormy sea and now come into quiet waters, he stood amid its hush, conscious of his every footfall and the very intonations of his voice. Instinctively he immediately pitched his tones lower and drew himself to his full height when he traversed the marble floor that separated the bordering show cases.

Individuals counted for more here than they did outside—far more. A person who came into Burton and Norcross sensed whether his tie was awry or his shoes unshined, and so did everybody else. For if you entered the shop at all, you entered it deliberately. No one ever strolled or sauntered into Burton and Norcross. It wasn't that sort of place. You would no more have ambled aimlessly along its center aisle, frankly proclaiming to all the world your opinion of what it had to sell, than you would casually have invaded the Court of St. James or Windsor Castle. Ambling was not done there. Nobody ambled. Even Mr. Burton himself didn't. Although he was the senior partner and could have claimed the privilege of ambling had he chosen, the shop transformed him just as it did everybody else. Once within its portals he became more erect, more commanding—in fact, a different human being altogether—and proceeded to announce right and left in accents never employed by him anywhere else that it was a beautiful day.

On this particular morning Christopher, who tagged meekly at his heels, fervently subscribed to the sentiment he advanced. It was a beautiful day. Almost any day, so new in the adventure of setting forth for a peep into the business world, would have seemed beautiful. And yet there was really nothing very novel in going to the store, for since a small boy he had been accustomed to being taken there to meet his father.

Sometimes such excursions culminated in new shoes or a new overcoat; sometimes in a pair of skates or in luncheon; and on a very red-letter day, such as a birthday or anniversary of some sort, in a matinée or moving-picture show.

Therefore Christopher was no stranger either to the plush-lined cases and their sparkling contents or to the men who presided over them. Everybody knew him by sight—doormen, salesmen, elevator boys, watchmakers, bookkeepers, and messengers. He was the son of the boss, Christopher Mark Antony Burton, fourth.

There were, alas, times when Christopher wished from the bottom of his heart he had been less well known. To be regarded as the future heir to all this splendor kept those he met in the establishment painfully deferential and created an estranging gulf 'twixt him and all that was human and interesting.

If, for example, when he bobbed unexpectedly into the elevator, old Joseph, its colored operator, had only kept right on munching an apple instead of whisking it out of sight into his pocket, how much pleasanter it would have been! Then, too, the men all insisted on calling him *sir*, which embarrassed him and made him feel very young and foolish. He had never desired to be a person of privilege for in spite of his sonorous name, Christopher was very democratic.

Probably if left to himself he would within twenty-four hours have been on the friendliest of terms with everybody in the shop. But in the background loomed his father of whom every employee stood in awe, and whose imposing presence they never forgot for one instant. You did not forget Mr. Christopher Mark Antony Burton, third, senior partner of the firm; he did not let you.

It was for this reason that Christopher the fourth made his

advent into the great shop with less joy and abandon than he would have done had conditions been otherwise. He was politely welcomed but not cordially. That would not have been fitting.

"Now what will you do to amuse yourself, son?" inquired Mr. Burton, after Tim had bowed them in the front door and called the elevator. "You are to please yourself. I shall be too busy to give a thought to you."

"Oh, I don't expect to be entertained," returned Christopher brightly. "Don't have me on your mind at all. I'll look after myself."

"That's right! That's right!" exclaimed his father, as if relieved by the intelligence. "You are welcome to go anywhere you like. Everybody knows you by sight and understands you are to be around here for a while. Just don't get into mischief. And see you are ready promptly at one to go to luncheon with me."

"You can count on me for that!"

"I'll wager I can."

With these words Mr. Burton opened the door of his office and disappeared.

Christopher hung up his hat and coat and hesitated uncertainly for a moment. He did not really know what he wanted to do. A general atmosphere of business of which he became instantly aware made him feel like an intruder. The men greeted him, it is true, but with minds focused far less on the salutation than on the various missions that drove them hither and thither.

There was something almost ludicrous about the seriousness with which they took this matter of rings and necklaces. One would have thought the affairs of a nation occupied them, so anxious and hurried were they.

He sauntered along the balcony in the wake of a red-cheeked young clerk who had bowed to him pleasantly and looked less as if he were speeding to save a burning ship or warn the king he was about to be blown up than did some of the others; and when this guide turned into a long, brilliantly lighted room, Christopher, having nothing better to do, entered too.

"You haven't finished that bracket clock yet, have you, McPhearson?" called the salesman, approaching a little old man who with a microscope to one eye was bending over a bench littered with small steel tools.

"Not yet, Bailey," the clockmaker replied without, however, looking up. "She's a queer piece, that clock—not one for ordinary treatment."

"But you can put her in shape, can't you?" came a bit anxiously from Bailey.

At the words a slow smile puckered the Scotchman's lips and for the first time he stole a glance at the speaker.

"Don't fret, Bailey," he drawled.

"I'm not fretting, Mr. McPhearson. But the woman who owns that clock won't sleep nights until she gets it home again."

"I don't blame her," was all McPhearson said.

"It's a good one, eh?"

"It's a dandy. I'd give my head for one like it. Genuine from start to finish and listed in the book. It was made by Richard Parsons of Number 15 Goswell Street, London, somewhere about 1720—at least he is down as a member of the Clockmakers' Company right along then. Pity he can't know his handiwork is still doing duty. He'd be proud of it. Two hundred years or more isn't a bad record for a clock."

"Two hundred years!" gasped Christopher involuntarily.

McPhearson peeped up over his microscope.

"This is Mr. Burton's son, McPhearson," put in Bailey.

"I know, I know. I've seen him round here ever since he could toddle. Good morning, youngster. So you've come to explore the repairing department, have you?"

The informality of the greeting was delightful to Christopher, and immediately his heart went out to the old Scotchman.

"I guess so, yes," smiled he. "I didn't know I was going to though. It just happened."

"It's not a bad happen, perhaps. Make yourself at home, laddie. Here's a stool."

"I'd rather stand and watch you."

"But I sha'n't let you. It makes me nervous to have somebody hanging over my shoulder and maybe jogging my elbow. If you're to stay you must sit," was the brusque but not unkindly answer.

Somewhat crestfallen the boy slipped to the stool and for a few moments remained immovable, watching the workman's busy fingers. How carefully they moved—with what fascinating deftness and rapidity!

"I see you are not one to keep hitching and twiddling around," the clockmaker presently remarked, with a twinkle. "We shall get on famously together. I detest nervous people."

"Are you fixing the clock Mr. Bailey was asking about?" Christopher ventured.

"Not just now, sonny. I am finishing up a simpler job. I shall go back to her in a minute, however. You can't just tinker her at will as you do common clocks. She has to be dreamed over."

"Dreamed over!" repeated Christopher, not a little puzzled.

"Aye, dreamed over! Well-nigh prayed over—if it comes to that," continued the old man gravely. "She isn't the sort that was turned out in a factory, you see, along with hundreds of others of her kind. She's an aristocrat and must be treated accordingly."

"Do you mean it—*she*—was made by hand?"

"Every wheel and rivet of her!"

"But I thought the works of all clocks were alike," asserted Christopher.

"Bless your heart, no. Nowadays most of them are; and there are advantages in it too, for when a part gives out, you can easily get another to replace it. But years ago in the days of the clockmakers' guilds, clocks were made by hand and were frequently entirely the work of one man—except perhaps the case, which was sometimes made by a joiner."

"Oh!"

"This old bracket clock, for instance, that I was speaking of—a fellow named Richard Parsons, who belonged to the London Clockmakers' Company between 1690 and 1730, made her from start to finish. You will see his name painted on the dial, and engraved on the works is his address. The jealous old clockmakers kept their eye on those who were manufacturing clocks, I can tell you. They weren't going to have a lot of cheap, poorly made articles shunted off on the public to ruin their trade. No, indeed. A man must serve a long apprenticeship before he could be admitted to the Clockmakers' Company and once enrolled must put his address in all his clocks so everybody would know he had a right to make and sell them."

"It wasn't a bad idea."

"Not at all bad. Nevertheless, the clockmakers were a stern, tyrannical lot. Nobody within twenty miles of London was allowed to make a clock unless enrolled in their organization. Moreover, they got from the king a right of search which enabled them to go in and seize any goods which they suspected fell below the standard. Not only did they want to be sure no poor clocks were made but they also wished to keep the monopoly of all the timepieces turned out.

"For example, when war in France drove many of the French

artisans to England, up rose the London clockmakers to protest against any of the French makers practicing their craft within their domains. Fortunately the petition was denied and at length these skilled workmen were enrolled in the company and together with their descendants gave to England some of her most beautiful clocks. But the old guild members did not suffer it without a wrench, I can tell you."

McPhearson took up a small screwdriver and proceeded to fasten the back on to the clock he held in his hand.

"It wasn't all smooth sailing, being a clockmaker in those days," he declared. "What wonder the horologers were jealous of their art? Just remember there were no factories to produce for you the screws, rivets, wheels, and parts you needed. You yourself had to make everything with the scant supply of tools at your command, usually a file, drill, and hammer. With these you hammered out your brass wheels to the required thickness, notched the teeth in their edges with the file, and fitted them into place. And when you consider that with this crude equipment you were expected to turn out a mechanism delicate enough to tell time, I am sure you will agree the stern old clockmakers had something on their side."

"They sure had!" Christopher exclaimed with enthusiasm.

"It is a glory to this Richard Parsons' skill that two hundred years after he made his clock it is still accurately performing its task. If anything I made was in existence at the end of a like stretch of time and was continuing to be useful, I should feel I had a right to be proud, shouldn't you?"

"You bet I would. Nothing I make ever stays together more than a week."

The Scotchman laughed at the boyish confession.

"Now you can understand, I guess, why I sent Bailey away,

telling him I should have to dream over this bracket clock. Two hundred years is a long time and methods have changed greatly since then. Therefore in order to repair such a product, I shall have to think myself back into the year 1700 and work in the fashion Richard Parsons did; otherwise I cannot successfully take up his handiwork. A clockmaker has to have imagination, you see."

"I never thought of that."

"It is such puzzles as these that make my trade interesting," McPhearson observed. "If every clock that came to me was of precisely the same pattern as every other, the work I do would be monotonous enough. But it is because clocks are as different as people that they pique my curiosity. Even those turned out in factories, for example, are never twice alike."

"I should think those would *have* to be alike," Christopher responded.

"You'd think so, and so would I if I had not handled so many and learned otherwise. No, every clock has its personality, its little tricks. One doesn't like a cold room, perhaps, and as a protest will stop or lose time; another shows its disapproval of the heat by being ten minutes fast. Still another balks at an incline in the mantelpiece, so slight that nobody can see it, and will not tick even. So it goes. And it is not always the most expensive clocks and watches, either, that keep the best time, for sometimes a cheap affair will, for reasons not to be fathomed, put to shame your costly one. Not infrequently I take to pieces a fine clock or watch and fail to find anything the matter with it, and yet it will not go as it should. The creatures actually seem to be stubborn and take notions just as people do."

"I'd no idea clocks were like that," mused Christopher.

"That's because you haven't lived with them more than half

a century as I have," the old man returned in friendly fashion. "I've summered and wintered them, you see, for fifty years and know their tricks and their manners. But this clock of Richard Parsons has no such caprices. It is a fine, sensible clock that goes faithfully about its business unless hindered by the lack of a rivet or a drop of oil. Just now its chimes are bothering; but we'll have them right after a little."

"Has it chimes?"

"Aye, surely. It has eight bells, though it is a small clock for the table or mantelpiece. The people of 1700 loved music and so did the clockmakers. Therefore clocks like this, that would play a different tune every day of the week, were in great demand. Maybe you never happened to see an old bracket clock of the long ago."

"No, I never did." Christopher shook his head.

"I'll go and fetch it. To tell you the truth, I put it away so it shouldn't be a temptation to me. Otherwise I'd be fussing with it and letting commonplace things such as this go."

McPhearson rose and shuffled away, only to return a few moments later carrying the bracket clock by its brass handle.

"So you never saw an old fellow like this, eh?" inquired he with evident satisfaction.

"No. I certainly never saw a clock with a brass handle on top to carry it by," confessed Christopher.

"And what do you say to its glass back and its beautifully chased works?" McPhearson turned his treasure round. "It was made to set on a table you see, or before the mirror that hung above the fireplace, in either of which spots the back of it would show almost as much as the front. Therefore its works were engraved, that one side should be quite as pleasing as the other."

"It's a beauty, isn't it?"

"SO YOU NEVER SAW AN OLD FELLOW LIKE THIS, EH?"

"Well, you won't see many like it," the Scotchman asserted proudly. "Not but what a good number of them were turned out in England between 1670 and 1750. But that was a long while ago, and things get scattered and are crowded out by newer fashions; besides, antique clocks are not always cared for and kept running. Then, too, it isn't always possible to find people who understand repairing such old fellows," McPhearson explained modestly. "As I said, they have to be taken as special cases and no end of thought put into them. More clocks are ruined by ignorant doctoring than by anything else. This one, thank goodness, has evidently always had intelligent care; if it hadn't it would not be ticking now."

Gently the man put his burden on the workbench.

It was a square clock with arched top and brass feet; and its face, suggesting that of a grandfather clock, was quaintly decorated with garlands of red roses. It had beautifully pierced hands, small brass cherub's heads at the corners, and at the top a single small hand pointed to its musical repertoire which consisted of: cotillion, jig, minuet, song, air, dance, and hymn.

"You can take your choice of tunes, you see," explained McPhearson. "There is one for every day of the week. All you have to do is to shift the indicator round to what your want to hear. It chimes every three hours—at six, nine, twelve, and three o'clock, and just before the music begins, it strikes one to indicate the hour."

"I wish I could hear it play."

"You shall by and by. And you may select the tune if you like. It has a pretty tone, something like that of a music box; and the selections are pretty, too—old-fashioned airs that were familiar to the people of that day and are now curious and interesting.

I want you to notice the brass spandrels while you are about it, for it is those that do much in helping us determine the dates when old clocks were made."

"I'm afraid I don't know what a spandrel is," Christopher announced with appealing frankness.

"And what marvel? How should you?" his companion replied pleasantly. "You have been such a good listener that I was forgetting you had not been brought up among clocks as I have been. Well, a spandrel is the small brass ornament at the corner that fills in the triangular gap left between the circular face and the square outline of the case. Some clocks have four of these, others such as this one only two. These ornaments were roughly cast in brass and afterward more carefully lacquered and finished by the clockmaker himself. Sometimes, however, we find them crudely executed as if they had been taken direct from the mold. Clockmakers of that time were not so inventive as we; neither had they had training in design, and as a result we see little variety in these brass ornamentations. At one period all these spandrels took the form of cherub's heads, an idea that may possibly have been copied from the Italians. Later a pattern with two cherubs supporting a crown was popular; and at a still later date the head of the cherub set in a scroll is found. That is the pattern on this one. The brass basketwork across the top is a relic of the old bird-cage clock which just preceded this one, and was cast by the metalsmith and then purchased by the clockmaker as were the spandrels.

"Since we know the approximate date that such metal work was done and have in addition Richard Parsons' name listed among the London Clockmakers' Company together with his address, there is pretty positive evidence that this antique is genuine."

"Was a list of all the London clockmakers kept?" questioned Christopher incredulously.

"Of those who belonged to the Clockmakers' Company, yes; but there were many excellent makers who lived in the country and therefore did not belong to this guild. Those who were members were, you may be moderately certain, fine workmen. For that matter you may rest assured that any old clock of early make which is still doing duty is a good clock; it would not be going now if it weren't."

"Of course. But Richard Parsons was really in the list, was he?"

"He was; his name, address, date of apprenticeship and the name of the maker to whom he was apprenticed; also the dates when he was admitted to the most worshipful Clockmakers' Company. So you see, although he lived long ago, Richard Parsons is no stranger to us."

"It makes you feel different when you know who he was, doesn't it?" commented Christopher slowly.

"Yes, and his work helps us to know a good deal about him too, for no lazy, careless person turned out such a clock as this. We must nevertheless take into consideration that in 1700 men had the leisure for careful handiwork. Nobody was in a hurry in those days. Richard Parsons, in his shop at Number 15 Goswell Street, had all the time in the world to make his clock, and could fuss about and experiment to his heart's content. Probably no one ever thought of jogging him on or pestering him to know if his work wasn't done."

Ruefully McPhearson shrugged his shoulders.

"Now I couldn't make a clock even were I so minded," he continued with a whimsical smile. "Mr. Bailey and a score of others as anxious as he would be prancing in here every half-hour to find out when it would be finished. They would expect it to be made, wound up, and ticking, inside a week. It was not so in the days of Queen Anne." The Scotchman sighed, then added, "Sometimes I envy them their leisure."

Once more he turned the clock round so Christopher could see its old-fashioned face gay with dainty vines and flowers.

"I declare if it isn't almost twelve o'clock," ejaculated he. "It's only three minutes behind schedule to-day. Still we must get it down finer than that. Besides, I'd rather it gained than lost time; losing is a grievous fault. Now what selection shall we play? Choose quickly for there isn't much leeway—"

"I'll have the dance."

"On with the dance!" McPhearson exclaimed gayly.

Opening the door at the front he moved the single hand until it pointed to the air desired. And he was none too soon, for an instant later the clock struck the hour and then, after a short pause, Christopher heard the tinkle of bells, thin, clear, and sweet, beginning to play a quaint snatch of melody. It was not at all the sort of dance music the boy had expected. Instead it was a merry little tune so gay one could not but be glad that noontide had come and that the sun rode high in the heavens.

"Jove, but that's jolly!" cried Christopher with delight. "I wish it would play right over again. If I had a clock like that I should run to listen to it every time it struck."

"That is what our men here did at first," laughed McPhearson. "They all threw down their tools and rushed here like a pack of children."

"Couldn't anybody buy one of these clocks?"

"I'm afraid were you to try to, you would find it would cost a small fortune," answered the Scotchman. "Once you could have secured such an article at a very modest price; but values increase with time, and to-day the work of Richard Parsons and those like him is at a premium. Moreover, old bracket clocks are not often for sale. Those who own them are aware of their value and will not part with them."

"Then I guess all I can do is to listen to this one," sighed Christopher.

"That is all I can do myself," McPhearson declared, with a wan smile. "I should consider I had a fortune could I own a treasure like this. But at least if I cannot own it, I can have the fun of keeping it running and there is some satisfaction in that."

"I should think there'd be a lot!" cried Christopher.

CHAPTER III
CHRISTOPHER ESCAPES BEING A HERO

L EAVING the repairing department, Christopher strolled to the edge of the balcony and idly looked down. Below all was bustle and brilliancy. Brass, copper, silver, and jewels flashed in the light of the galleries beneath him, which despite the fact that Thanksgiving was barely over, were already astir with the vanguard of Christmas shoppers. Far down on the main floor he could see men and women in eager consultation over Colonial silver, Sheffield trays, gay-colored feather fans and multi-hued parasols.

For quite an interval he watched, deriving no small degree of amusement from the uncertainty, anxiety, animated gestures and helpless bewilderment of some of the less inspired of the visitors; then, wearying of this entertainment, he descended by the stairway to the third and afterward to the second gallery, where he again paused to lean over the carved rail and obtain a closer view of the panorama.

It chanced that just beneath him was a long showcase filled with gems before which two gentlemen in fur coats were standing, earnestly conversing with the salesman. On the counter lay a tray of rings and these one of the men was trying on and examining. It was plain from the clerk's eager manner that his prospective purchaser was wavering between two costly articles, neither one of which quite suited him. With desperate earnestness the salesman pleaded, cajoled, and argued, and unconsciously Christopher, looking down, became almost as interested as he to see what would come of the matter.

The taller man slipped a band of diamonds on his finger, turned it round, held the hand it graced at arm's length, then frowned, took off the ring, and tried the other.

Meantime his friend was called on for his opinion and advised sympathetically. Christopher pursed his lips scornfully. The two were like a pair of vain old peacocks and silly as women, thought he. How foolish for men to be wearing jewels, anyway. You wouldn't catch him arrayed in a big diamond ring. And the strangest part of it was that the man who was thus frittering away his money did not look at all like a fop but was tall, muscular, and had a scar, not unlike a sword cut, across his right cheek. It was a strange mark that ran from his ear almost to the corner of his mouth, and it gave his face a disagreeable, sinister expression.

His comrade was less robust—a small, wiry fellow, who seemed lost in the heavy coat he wore. In spite of the heat of the room, he had not turned down his collar, which all but concealed his face, and once Christopher noticed that he leaned surreptitiously forward and drew that of his companion higher about his ears. Thus they dallied, laughing, joking, objecting, until the distracted clerk, fearful lest he lose such promising customers, was well-nigh out of his wits. It seemed as if they never would be suited, and at last, suddenly inspired, the salesman dashed off to the farther end of the show case in evident search for something he had forgotten to show them.

It was during the instant he was thus occupied that Christopher saw, or thought he saw, the taller of the men wrench the ring he was wearing from his finger, drop it inside his glove, and substitute for it one his companion handed him. The exchange—if exchange it was—took place in a flash and was over so quickly the boy could scarcely believe his eyes. A second later the clerk returned triumphantly, displayed another ring, and renewed his attentions without noticing anything amiss. But his purchasers shook their heads, pushed the rings aside, and moved away.

Then, and not until then, was Christopher urged to action. He awakened as out of a dream, wondering whether what he had witnessed was real, and if it was, what he ought to do. The two fur-coated gentlemen were almost at the door. If he was to do anything at all, it must be now. Fortunately a stairway was at no great distance; and he raced down it as fast as his feet would carry him. When he reached the street floor, the door had, alas, closed on the suspected thieves. It came to him now how much wiser it would have been had he shouted from the balcony, instead of waiting to descend. If he had done that the men might have been stopped before they got away. But it was all so unbelievable that he hadn't the nerve to cry out. Had he been mistaken, a pretty sort of fool he would have appeared; besides, he had not thought of it. His bright ideas always seemed to come afterward.

Well, at any rate he was alert enough now. It took him no time to rush up to the perspiring clerk, who, discouraged, stood mopping his brow, and gasp:

"Those men—one of them took a ring—I saw him."

"*What!*"

"He did. He put it in his glove."

"But the rings are all here."

"It was another one," panted Christopher. "His friend slipped it to him and he—"

The salesman paled. Breathlessly he dragged out the tray of rings and pounced upon one of them.

"My soul!" he faltered weakly. "You're right. It's a fake. There's no mark on it. Ring, Grant! Ring that bell for the detective. The 'phone—quick—and call headquarters! We'll put somebody on their track as fast as ever we can." Then, turning to Christopher, he shouted accusingly, "Why in the deuce didn't you sing out before they got away? And where were you, anyhow, that you saw the affair?"

While the other clerks at the counter gathered round Christopher, he related exactly what he had witnessed.

"You'd know the chaps again?"

"I'd know the big one—I'm sure I should, because of the scar on his cheek."

"Scar? I didn't notice it," murmured the unhappy salesman. "I was too busy listening to their blarney, I guess. They meant I should be, too—idiot that I was. I can't see why you didn't sing out, kid." The clerk, thoroughly demoralized, had apparently entirely forgotten that Christopher was the son of the senior partner.

"I was too surprised! It was all so quick, you see. It almost seemed as if it hadn't happened," repeated the boy wretchedly.

"Why blame the boy, Hollings, when you yourself hadn't the wit to be on your guard?" put in the man called Grant.

"That's so! That's so!" moaned the unfortunate fellow.

"At least he has lost little time. He has given us pretty prompt warning and enabled us to get our nets out much sooner than we should have otherwise. But for him, you might not have discovered anything was wrong before night."

"I know. Yes, he's done a big service, certainly. But it would have been a bigger had he stopped the thieves before they made their get-away."

"There is no use to go back to that. Neither you nor I would, perhaps, have done better. Had he shouted from the balcony and accused two innocent customers of stealing, we should have been a sight worse off. The lad was just being prudent."

"Yes! Yes, he did the wise thing, I guess, since he wasn't sure."

"We cannot insult patrons without proof."

"No."

"Besides, if Master Christopher took good heed of the rascals and can help to identify them, he will do still further service."

"To be sure—yes—yes—of course," the distraught clerk answered. "But it is all very unfortunate. To think of their putting it over on me—me, who have been here twenty years and never lost an article. It's terrible!"

"Cheer up, Hollings."

"I shall lose my place," wailed Hollings. "Lose it as sure as the world. Wait until the boss hears of it."

"My father is never unjust," Christopher put in stoutly.

"Your father? I beg your pardon, Mr. Christopher. I'd forgotten you were here, sir. No, your father always does the square thing," Hollings hastened to declare. "But he'll not understand. He'll think I should have been more careful! And so I had—I won't deny it. But my wife and children—my God!"

"Come, come, Hollings," interrupted a newcomer, whom the group greeted as Mr. Rhinehart. "There's no good crying over spilled milk. We may get the ring back again, you know."

"Oh, do you think so?"

"There is a good chance of it. I have telephoned and headquarters has its nets set already. The pawnshops are watched and so are the roads out of the city. The police, too, have their orders. Any minute we expect the inspector to talk with you and this young gentleman here."

"With me?" Christopher exclaimed with a start.

"Surely! You're the hero of this adventure, son."

"Not much of a hero, I'm afraid."

"Well, you're the one who escaped being the hero, then," laughed Mr. Rhinehart. "At least, you know more of the affair than does anybody else."

"But I'd be scared to death of the inspector," faltered the boy.

"Pooh! He's only a man, sonny, like any other. You've nothing to fear from him, since you are on the right side of the fence. If you were on the wrong side, then indeed you might tremble."

"The inspector has arrived," a messenger from upstairs announced. "He is in Mr. Burton's office with the members of the firm. He wishes to see the house detective, the salesman, and young Burton."

"I guess I'm in for it," Hollings whispered to Mr. Rhinehart.

"Nonsense! Tell the truth—that's all you've got to do."

"But I was such a duffer!"

"I fumbled the ball, too, Mr. Hollings," interrupted Christopher consolingly. "Remember I didn't play a very brilliant game."

"The game wasn't up to you, sonny," Hollings returned. "It was I. I did the foozling."

Up they shot in the elevator.

The messenger in his uniform and buttons went ahead and opened the door.

"Mr. Hollings is here, sir," announced he. "And Mr. Christopher and the detective, Mr. Waldron."

As the three crossed the threshold and entered the office, Christopher saw Mr. Norcross and the inspector. A deep hush was upon the room. Not only did its occupants look grave—they looked severe—awesome. One glance and the lad did not wonder poor Hollings' knees knocked together. Mr. Norcross was imposing enough, but the inspector was even worse; and as for the senior partner of the firm—well, he was Mr. Christopher Mark Antony Burton, third, arrayed in his most awful dignity. Even his son trembled before him.

CHAPTER IV
AN ENCOUNTER WITH THE POLICE

AND so, Hollings," the great Mr. Burton began, "while your back was turned, you have lost some of our valuable diamonds."

"My back was not turned, sir," objected Hollings. "I merely looked away a minute."

"Long enough to give a pair of thieves the opportunity to work."

"It hardly seemed so."

"But it was."

"I'm afraid so, Mr. Burton. I am deeply sorry, sir; and yet had I it to do over again I hardly see—"

"It wasn't his fault, Dad—indeed it wasn't. I saw the whole thing, you know. It was done so fast you almost thought your eyes deceived you."

"Oh, the men were experts. There can be no questions about that!" cut in the deep voice of the inspector. "Now, Mr. Burton, instead of wasting time in reprimands, we've got to get down to facts. May I question these people?"

"Certainly, certainly!" Mr. Burton, however, seemed to be taken aback at being treated with such scant ceremony. "This is Mr. Hollings, the clerk; and this lad is my son, Christopher."

"Very good! Now, Mr. Hollings, suppose you tell your tale

first. Relate exactly what happened—not what you thought or supposed. Stick to facts."

"I will, sir."

In a trembling voice Hollings began his story, and as he recounted it, Mr. Inspector jotted it down, merely pausing now and then to ask a curt question.

"Can you describe the men?" inquired he, when the narrative was finished.

"I'm afraid I can't, sir, beyond the fact that both of them wore raccoon motoring coats, and kept their collars pretty well turned up. You see I was far too much occupied with what they were saying to consider how they looked."

"You could not identify them then?"

"Not positively—no, I regret to say I couldn't. I might possibly recognize the hand or the voice of the big man."

"The one who tried on the rings?"

"Yes, sir."

"But you could not pick him out from a group of others or identify him by photograph."

"No, I couldn't."

"That's a pity. In your work you should be more observing."

"I know I should. I will be in the future."

The inspector smiled grimly.

"We all lock the gate after the cows are out of the pasture," commented he. "Well, if this is all you can offer, I'll try the boy. Your name, sonny."

"Christopher Burton."

"Christopher Mark Antony Burton, fourth," interrupted his father in an aggrieved tone.

"Does all that belong to you?" asked the inspector, his eyes fixed on the lad's face with hawk-like scrutiny.

"I'm afraid it does."

"Afraid, Christopher!" Mr. Burton ejaculated. "Afraid! Why, it is a fine, honorable name. Your grandfather and your great-grandfather—"

"Suppose we omit his grandfathers for the present," said the inspector, unceremoniously putting an end to Mr. Burton's dissertation. "So that's your name, is it?"

"Yes, sir."

"Why didn't you give the whole of it at the beginning?"

"Oh, because there are such yards of it."

The inspector grinned.

"Now be good enough to tell us *your* version of this affair. Relate exactly what you saw, heard, and did."

"I'm afraid I didn't do much," protested Christopher sheepishly.

"You might have done more and I won't deny I wish to goodness you had. However, you acted with considerable sense. You might have done worse—much worse."

"I'm glad if you think so," the boy asserted modestly. "It seemed to me afterward that I had been very stupid. It all was so quick! Almost like sleight-of-hand."

"You were up against experts, sonny," Mr. Inspector remarked more gently than he had yet spoken. "You did well to detect them at all. Now fire ahead with your yarn."

In simple, straightforward fashion Christopher told his story and it was evident several parts afforded his critical listener satisfaction, for twice he muttered beneath his breath:

"Very good! *Very* good!"

The tale finished, Christopher paused, breathless.

"Could you give me any description of these fellows?" his cross questioner inquired.

"The big chap—the one who tried on the rings—was tall, heavy, had light hair and a bald spot on the top of his head. I looked right down on it."

"Excellent!"

"His eyes I could not see. His face was smooth-shaven, and on his right cheek, going from his ear almost to the corner of his mouth, was a white, queer sort of scar that—"

The inspector started from his seat, then sank back again.

"Ah!" was all he said. "And the other fellow?"

"Small, dark, black-haired, with a coat much too big for him. His nose was sharp, and he kept looking over his shoulder."

"Anything else?"

"I'm afraid that's all, except that his hands were dirty as if they had been in ink or grease or something. Maybe they hadn't, though."

The inspector beamed upon him.

"You have a very observing son, Mr. Burton, very! He's a fine lad. You should be proud of him."

"Has he helped you at all?"

"At all? He has given me precisely the information I was after."

"And you think you could identify the men?"

"I know them already."

"Know who they are?" gasped Christopher.

"Yes."

It was obvious the expert was enjoying the lad's mystification.

"You don't mean you know their names," persisted Christopher.

"Indeed I do—all their many names, for they have almost as long a list of them as you have yourself."

The inspector evidently considered this a good joke, for

he laughed heartily at it without noticing how the great Mr. Burton glared at him.

"And not only do I know their names, but I have their pictures as well," he continued, when he had done laughing. "What do you think of that?"

"Met them before, have you?" interrogated Mr. Burton, his disapproval mollified to some degree by his pride in his son.

"Oh, I know all about that pair," replied the inspector; "if they prove to be the couple I think them. No wonder your clerk failed to suspect them. They are very polished gentleman."

"They were indeed, sir," Hollings put in. "They had a million-dollar air about them."

"I know they had. They are crackajacks at this sort of thing. They are wanted this minute in Chicago for a job not unlike this one."

"Really!"

Christopher's face glowed with excitement. To think he had actually beheld two such desperate characters and given evidence against them! If he had only spoken sooner and helped to capture them!

Something of this regret probably shadowed his brow, for the inspector added:

"They would have managed their get-away even had you given the alarm, son. Both were doubtless well armed and prepared to make their escape. Taken by surprise, as you clerks all were, no one could have stopped them. They would have shot any person who obstructed their dash for liberty."

"Do you think so?" Poor Hollings drew a breath of relief.

"I know it. They've done it before. They had their pistols and a waiting motor car, and had no mind to be caught."

"Then if I'd yelled from the balcony—"

"It would have done no good and would, perhaps, have done much harm instead. You would merely have furnished an alarm on which they would instantly have acted. As it is, we know them, and our nets are out. I would, however, like to take your son down to headquarters, Mr. Burton, and let him look over our photographs just to see if he can pick these winners from the bunch."

"Certainly, sir. Certainly! Get your hat and coat, Christopher. I believe I'll go along too, Mr. Inspector, if you are willing. My son and I were just starting out to lunch."

"By all means; I have a car here."

"I don't suppose I could persuade you to—"

"No, thank you, Mr. Burton. I'm up to my ears in business, sir. However, you are very kind. I must get right back to head-quarters as fast as I can."

"I see."

"This is a detailed description of the ring, is it?" continued he, tapping an envelope he held in his hand. "Size of the diamonds, their weight, the complete record?"

"Yes."

"Good. I guess that's all we need."

"Do you think you will be able to—"

"To land the jewels, you mean? I can't tell you that, sir. It's too early in the game."

"I suppose so. It was a foolish question."

Evidently the inspector was of the same opinion, for he made no answer.

"Well, that's all, Hollings," announced the great man, turning to his clerk. "You may go now."

"I hope and pray the ring may be recovered, sir. I shall not have a happy moment until it is."

"All that must rest with the police. The case is in their keeping now," was his employer's terse reply.

In the meantime, Mr. Norcross had not said anything at all. He seldom did say anything. But as the group rose to depart, he dragged himself up out of his chair and, as if giving his blessing to the enterprise, remarked:

"Good luck to you, Inspector!"

"Thank you, sir."

Then Christopher, his father and the Chief entered the elevator and afterward the car that took them to headquarters.

Here the boy had displayed before him an array of photographs from which he had not the slightest trouble in picking that of the man with the scar; but his sharp-nosed companion he was unable to identify.

"I thought I'd recognize him anywhere," lamented Christopher. "His hair was so black and thick that—"

At the words, the inspector jumped a little.

"Ha!" exclaimed he. "Tony wore a wig, did he?" He opened a drawer. "Any of these look like him?"

He passed to Christopher a handful of pictures.

"There he is," cried the lad presently, choosing one out of the lot. "There he is! Only he didn't have his glasses on."

"I fancy he isn't dependent on them all the time," chuckled the inspector. "Well done, my boy. Yes, that's Tony when he's dressed up. The reason you didn't recognize him was because in the other picture he wasn't. Clothes do not make the man, but wigs, glasses, and things change him a good deal. That's all, gentlemen. I now have all the information I wish, and need not detain you."

"I suppose I shall be notified when any news is obtained," said Mr. Burton, rising. He wasn't used to being dismissed in this curt fashion. When any dismissing was to be done, it was usually he who did it.

"Yes, sir. As soon as anything definite is known. *Good* morning!" But to Christopher he reached out a detaining hand. "You've done uncommonly well, sonny," he whispered. "Don't worry because you didn't land the chaps. I'm only thankful you didn't give them the chance to shoot you. We'll have the birdies yet."

"Shall I have to go to court?"

"Court? Perhaps. But, Lord! A boy that can tell as straight a story as you needn't fear that. It's not half as bad as being stood up to face me."

"I didn't mind you at all."

"I'm glad of that. I don't want my job to turn me into an ogre. There are people who don't feel that way about me." He laughed slyly. "Don't you fret about being haled into court. Several persons besides ourselves wish to meet those two distinguished gentlemen we are after. When we get them they will have to be shipped to Chicago and various other cities. You stand a slim chance of having any very extensive acquaintance with them."

The voice of Mr. Burton, who was loitering impatiently outside, was now heard calling:

"Christopher! Christopher!"

"That's your dad. He's getting tired of cooling his heels in the corridor. He isn't used to it. Better trot along, sonny. Somebody might mistake him for a questionable character and run him in."

The inspector's hearty "Haw, haw!" lent to his laughter the suspicion that he found something intensely humorous about Mr. Christopher Mark Antony Burton, third, senior partner of the firm of Burton and Norcross.

CHAPTER V
CHRISTOPHER ASTONISHES HIMSELF

IT does not take long for news to travel, and when Christopher entered the shop the next morning it was to find himself quite a hero. On every hand clerks saluted him with such greetings as:

"Well, how is Sherlock Holmes to-day?"

"Have you been landing any more bandits, Mr. Christopher?"

"Joined the secret service yet, Master Christopher?"

Poor Christopher, who was none too proud of the part he had played, was a good deal abashed; nevertheless he tried to accept the banter cheerfully, perceiving that it was kindly intentioned. But the glory of it paled at last, and, weary of such jests, he fled to seek out McPhearson, who, he felt sure, would offer him no flattery.

The Scotchman was so busy toiling over the bracket clock with the chimes that he did no more than glance up when the boy dropped down on the stool opposite.

"I hear you did a pretty bit of work yesterday," he at last remarked.

"No, I didn't. On the contrary I was darn stupid. I had the chance to be a hero, but I muffed it."

"They didn't seem to think so downstairs," was the clock-maker's laconic retort.

"Oh, I didn't do much of anything, honest I didn't, Mr. McP-hearson. I just happened along at the right time—or, perhaps—at the wrong," explained the boy with an embarrassed laugh.

"Apparently it was decidedly at the wrong," observed the old man, continuing to file with extreme care a bit of brass he held between his fingers.

Christopher watched, admiring the speed and skill of his gnarled fingers.

"How's she getting along?" ventured he after a long silence.

"She's about O. K. now. Running fine—I'm just tinkering the catch on the door, for even Richard Parsons cannot coax things into wearing forever. She'll go home to-day."

There was a sigh from the Scotchman.

"I do believe you're sorry to be done with her," asserted the boy mischievously. A second later, however, he regretted his impulsive jest, for his companion answered gravely:

"I am. I've enjoyed working on her. I'd be far sorrier, though, did I not know she is going where she will be appreciated. The woman that owns her watches over her as if she were a live creature—and indeed she is—almost."

"It's nice to feel she isn't being wasted on some dumbbell, isn't it?" declared Christopher, catching the old man's enthusiasm.

"She's not being wasted. I can answer for that. I know the house where she lives well, for I've been there times without number to regulate clocks. There are some beauties and they have the history of every one of them—the name of the maker, the date when they were made, the place, and all. I like to handle clocks for people like that. It shows they are intelligent and care. Some folks do not know one thing about their clocks. They won't even take the trouble to wind them regularly. Neverthe-less they are the first ones to fuss if the poor things fail to keep good time. I wonder how they would like, for example, to have their meals served to them just whenever somebody happened to think of it."

Christopher nodded agreement with the sentiment.

"To be sure," McPhearson continued, "people sometimes own clocks that aren't worth much pains. Still, it's only right to keep them cleaned and help them to do the best they can, even at that. All clocks can't be Tompions, or Grahams, or Quares, any more than we can all be Washingtons and Lincolns. It isn't their fault nor ours."

"You care a lot about clocks, don't you?" meditated Christopher aloud.

"I suppose I do," the old man confessed. "Clocks have come to be almost people to me; in fact, some of them are a good sight better than people. By that, I mean they have finer traits. They go quietly ahead and do their work without bluster or complaint. When they don't it is usually because something's the matter with them. They are patient, faithful, useful, and were they to be taken out of the world they would be terribly missed and would leave it a pretty higgledy-piggledy place."

"I guess there is no danger of the world being without clocks," returned Christopher comfortably. "There seem to be plenty to go round."

"But there weren't always plenty," broke in McPhearson quickly. "You chance to live in a fortunate age, young man, and do not half appreciate your blessings. Had you lived a few hundred years ago you would have had no clocks."

"Mercy on us! Why, how on earth did people manage to get on without them?"

"Primitive persons studied the sun and calculated by that," McPhearson responded. "Then some ingenious creature thought out the sundial whereby the hour could be gauged by a shadow; also marks were made where the sun would strike at a given time—perhaps at noon. Such a notch was called the noon mark."

"Oh, gee! But suppose there was no sun?"

"Exactly! Now you have put your finger on the pulse of the dilemma! What was to be done when there was no sun? The sundial at best was none too correct. In different latitudes, too, different markings were needed. Moreover, a sundial, to be of practical value, had to be kept steady. What was to happen on shipboard? On cloudy days? At night?"

"The sundial was about as much good as a fan would be in Greenland," grinned Christopher.

"Yes, just about. It was these sunless hours that were the problem."

"Humph! I never thought of that in my life."

"Most of us don't."

"I suppose that was why people began making clocks."

"You don't for a moment imagine men leaped from sundials to clocks, do you?" interrogated the Scotchman quizzically.

"Oh, perhaps not such nice ones as ours,' conceded the boy with easy unconcern. "Still they had to tell time somehow."

"Clocks were a long way off from suns and shadows."

"But what did come next?"

"To sundials, you mean? Well, for a long, long time people could think of nothing better. They introduced trifling remedies now and then, however. For example, in the seventeenth century they evolved a portable dial that could be carried from place to place. Sometimes this was combined with a compass; sometimes it was made in the form of a ring. It was an awkward substitute for the watch, but it was, nevertheless, great-great-great-grandfather to it. Yet advantageous as it was to be able to carry the time about with you, it did nothing to lessen the long, unmarked stretch of darkness that descended upon the earth every night. How was man to solve that difficulty?"

"How indeed?"

"That was his puzzle—his nut to crack. Throughout the ages it has been conundrums like these that have taxed human ingenuity and made of life such an alluring adventure. On the conquering of difficulties civilization has been built up. Well, man now attacked this problem of telling time. He did not aspire to narrow it down to any very fine point, for at that period of history one day was very like another, and he was a leisurely being with little to do but eat, sleep, fight or hunt. Notwithstanding this, however, he did want to know *when* it was noon; *when* it would be day. King Alfred, one of the English monarchs, hit upon a plan for telling the hours of the night by means of tall candles, made to burn a definite interval. When, for example, one of his candles burned out, he knew that four or six hours had passed. Other persons went further and had candles marked off into hours with black and white wax—"

"That was a clever scheme!"

"Clever, yes; and all very well for kings who could afford to burn wax tapers night after night. But there were, alas, many unfortunates who couldn't. Accordingly the obstacle persisted, and urged the world on to the next step up the time-telling ladder."

"And what was that?" demanded Christopher with interest.

"Telling time by water."

"By *water*! But how?"

"It was not so difficult as it sounds. In reality it was quite a simple plan. The ancients would take a jar, make a tiny hole in the bottom of it, fill it with water, and let the water drip slowly out. Having measured how long it would take to empty the jar, they had a sort of water clock."

"Bravo! That was certainly easy."

"Easy and far better than the sundial, too, for water would drip either in light or darkness, on cloudy days as well as bright ones. By means of marks on the jar, shorter intervals of time could also be determined. The receptacle, however, had to be kept filled and the hole free so there should be no variation in the regularity of the dripping. This water clock was called a *clepsydra*, the name being taken from two Greek words meaning 'thief of water.' Well, as you may imagine, the populace were delighted with this contrivance. It seemed as if now they certainly had the prize for which they had been searching. Moreover, with the water clock a new factor in time came into being. Instead of telling *when*, as the sundial did, the clepsydra, by measuring a given interval, told *how long*, which was a very different thing indeed. In other words it began to draw people's attention to the duration of time."

"That is different, isn't it?" mused the boy.

"Quite another matter altogether," McPhearson said. "Immediately the Athenians, who had invented the device, put it to work and proceeded to limit the length of time speakers should talk in their courts of justice. Evidently then, as now, men were fond of making speeches and arguing and became so fascinated by hearing themselves talk that they forgot to stop. Now here was something that would put a check on them. When a case came up for a hearing, the accuser was allowed the first jar of water, the accused the second, and the judge the third. Stationed beside the clepsydra was a special officer whose duty it was not only to fill it but to stop the flow whenever a speaker was interrupted, thereby making certain he was not cheated of any of the time due him."

"A bully scheme!" Christopher remarked.

"It worked," McPhearson answered. "With such strict rules you may be sure there was none of the thing the Athenians termed 'babbling.' Men guarded their words like jewels when each word meant the dripping away of his allotted time."

"And did people continue to use this water clock?"

"Yes, for quite a time, but after a while they began to find fault with it. In the first place they noticed that when the vessel was full the greater pressure of water caused it to drip much faster than when there was not much in it. This they had not considered before, and the discovery forced them to attempt to improve it. This they did by concocting a sort of double jar. In the lower one there was a float that rose as the container filled; and since the top one was constantly replenished, it kept the pressure in the bottom one uniform."

"The best yet!"

"Much the best. In fact it was a stride ahead from several standpoints, for although it could not really be termed a machine it nevertheless was a device that did for man something he would otherwise have had to do for himself, which is the aim of all machinery. In just that proportion he moved toward a civilization where artificial methods relieved him of his labor. Thus he advanced quite a distance from that primitive condition when he did everything with his hands toward his next state of fashioning tools that would do what he wished to do better and quicker; here was something which worked independently of him."

"Why, so it was! I never thought before that man passed through those three stages," ejaculated Christopher with pleasure; "it makes our old forefathers twice as interesting, doesn't it?"

"Three times as interesting," the Scotchman laughingly

responded. "Facts make very delightful stories, if you fasten them together. Scattered, unrelated information is both dry and worthless. It is only when linked up in the chain of history that it becomes interesting and valuable."

"The trouble with me is I never know where the things I learn belong," observed the lad soberly. "It's like fitting pieces into a puzzle when you've no notion what picture you are making."

"I know, sonny," returned the old man with sympathy. "But do not imagine you are the only one who is not always able to put in the proper place the scraps of knowledge in his possession. Many an older person has wondered what part his learning had in the gigantic total of the ages. World history is conceived on a pretty big scale, you see. But that all we glean is somehow linked up with the rest, you may be very sure. Certainly this clepsydra was."

"It's easy enough to see that *afterward*," asserted Christopher. "And so the Greeks managed to fix up their water clock to their satisfaction, after all."

"Alas, not wholly to their satisfaction," was the answer, "for presently other difficulties concerning it arose. For example, unless the water poured into it was absolutely clean, the hole would fill up and the drip become slower; moreover, you must consider what happened in cold weather, for not only were these water clocks in unheated buildings, but you will recall they were set up in the market place or public square so the villagers might consult them. Here assembled the watch, whose duty it was to patrol the town and blow a horn for the changing of the guard; here, too, was stationed the officer whose duty it was at stated hours to refill the clepsydra."

"Oh, I suppose the darn thing froze—that probably was the next obstacle," grinned Christopher.

"It was," nodded McPhearson.

"Then it couldn't have been much better than the old sundial," the lad sniffed, with contempt.

"It had its outs. Nevertheless it held the front of the stage about two thousand years, and then I am sure you will agree it was high time a better device was substituted."

"And what was that?"

"The sand glass."

"Our hourglass, you mean?"

"Yes—or half-hour, quarter-hour—any fraction of an hour you choose. The idea of the sand glass was not entirely new, because some form of running sand had long before been used in the Far East. But the sand glass as we know it was new to the European world, and you cannot but agree it was a far more practical article than was the clepsydra for it neither froze nor had to be replenished. Moreover, it was lighter, less bulky, and could be carried about, and the old water clocks could not—that is, not without great inconvenience and danger of breaking. Oh, the sand glass was vastly better! Even now, after all these years, it is not entirely out of date, for it is still used to mark definite intervals of time."

"I have one at home to practice by."

"Many persons use them," the clockmaker averred. "It is not unusual to have speakers limit their addresses by them. In fact, a two-minute glass is still employed in the House of Commons and until 1839 the British Navy measured the watch on shipboard by a glass that ran an hour and a half. The marking off of time in such definite lengths as this, however, did not take place in ancient times. At that period people seldom attempted fine measurements of the day. The problem of hours, minutes, seconds, and fractions of them was something they scarcely dreamed of. Nor did they need to cut their time up into such small parts. Life, as I before remarked, was not very rushing. Nobody expected to meet anybody else at a particular instant in those far-away, lazy, easy-going times, or to go anywhere on the minute. If you arrived at where you were going before the darkness fell that was all even the most ambitious asked. The splitting up of time with our present-day nicety is of comparatively modern working out."

"That seems funny, doesn't it?" Christopher suggested.

"Yes, until you see how naturally it grew out of an advancing civilization. After this slow-moving, sleepy interval of idleness and ignorance, when there were no books, no schools, no learning of any kind, there came a great waking up, or Renaissance, which stirred the populace in every direction. Printing was invented, books written, and people, hearing of other lands, began to travel. In consequence life became busier and time more valuable. Moreover, with the spread of Christianity, monasteries and convents were everywhere erected, and attached to these religious orders were specified intervals for work, prayer and various masses and services. Such periods were marked off by the ringing of bells. Thus it happened quite consistently that the first clocks introduced were in religious buildings and on the spires of churches and were without faces or hands, merely indicating by the stroke of one or more bells the termination of the hour."

"But I should not call that a clock at all," Christopher objected.

"Oh, it was a clock. Such a contrivance could not perform its function without works. The bell or bells rung as a result of turning wheels. Moreover, the very word 'clock' is derived from a root which in almost every language means 'bell.' The French was *cloche*, the Saxon *clugga*. Thus it came about that later on the works of more modern clocks frequently had two distinct mechanisms: the bell portion that chimed or struck the hour, and the section that included the moving of the hands. Years afterward we find this distinction still maintained, and discover old clockmakers speaking of a clock that did not strike merely as a *timekeeper*."

"How curious!" murmured Christopher. "And who was it that evolved this machine that would strike the hours?"

"That, I suppose, we shall never positively know; but in all probability it was a monk, who, having considerable leisure at his command and perhaps being held responsible for the ringing of the monastery bell once in so often, bethought himself of a scheme whereby the bell could be made to ring without him. History tells us that William, Abbott of Hirschau, who died toward the end of the eleventh century, invented a horologium modeled after the celestial hemisphere; therefore he may have been the inventor of the clock, for soon after his death these striking bells begin to make their appearance on church towers and in other religious buildings.

"A couple of centuries later we read of clocks being sent as presents. Sultan Saladin sent to Emperor Frederick II a very ambitious article which by means of weights and wheels not only indicated the hours but the course of the sun, moon, and planets. Now who invented such an affair as that we do not know. It must, however, have been some ingenious Saracen who certainly could have heard nothing about the Abbott of Hirschau and his striking bells. Indeed, when one considers the superstition of the age, we cannot but grant it was almost fortunate a clock such as ours was not then invented, for people were great believers in witchcraft and were liable to attribute to evil spirits anything they did not understand, and forthwith destroy it."

"How ridiculous!" scoffed Christopher.

"They were children, remember—intellectual children—ignorant as babies because, poor souls, they had had neither books nor teaching. Savages are, you know, terrified at a thing they cannot fathom and these persons were as yet little more. Well, at any rate, clocks began to make their appearance. By 1286 one of these faceless mechanisms was put up on St. Paul's Cathedral in London; and before 1300, others were, by order of the clergy, installed at Canterbury and Westminster."

"And these just chimed or struck?"

"That is all. On some was a single bell; on others crudely carved wooden figures beat out the hour on a series of bells. All these were known as 'clocks,' the term 'horologe' not yet being in common use."

"Horologe!" repeated Christopher slowly. "You don't suppose that word has anything to do with the Latin *hora*, meaning hour, do you?"

"I suppose it has a good deal," McPhearson returned with a dry smile.

"Really!" Plainly Christopher was delighted by this discovery. "Well, well! Old Cæsar, Esquire, isn't so bad, after all. *Hora!* I never expected to see the day that stuff would be of any earthly use."

"I told you all you needed to do with what you learn is to link it to something else."

"But I never seemed to be able to hook it on before," confided the lad frankly. "Gee, but it makes me chesty! I'm pleased to death with myself!"

To save himself the old Scotchman could not but chuckle at his companion's naïve satisfaction.

"Somehow it's a bit tough to get this linking-up idea just

when I can't do any more studying," added the boy a trifle wistfully.

"Oh, you will be back at school before long, son; and if you go back more eager to learn will that not be a gain?"

"Sure it will! *Hora!* Jove! I made a neat guess, didn't I? And that's where that horologium you were talking about came from, too. I'm not so worse. Miss Alden, my Latin teacher, would fall in a faint if she heard me rolling out these Latin derivatives, I'll bet. I'm not often taken this way. Say, Mr. McPhearson, I seem to be learning quite a lot if I'm not in school. This is a darn pleasanter way to do it, too."

CHAPTER VI
CLOCKS THAT WERE GOOD AS PLAYS

B Y the end of two weeks, school with its games and its bells for recitation had become a thing of the past and Christopher felt as much at home in his father's shop as if his name was inscribed upon its payroll.

Nevertheless, despite the lapse of time, no trace either of the missing gems or of the two diamond robbers had been secured. Both Mr. Burton and Mr. Norcross were beginning to be discouraged, and feared the culprits would never be captured; even Christopher's hope of seeing his adventure brought to a favorable climax was fading. As for poor Hollings, he was another man altogether and it seemed as if he would never be able to hold his head up again. A part of the value of the gems was, to be sure, covered by burglar insurance, and therefore the loss to the firm would not be great; rather it was the disgrace of the episode that bowed the salesman to the ground. He was an old and trusted employee who took the matter so hard that within the fortnight he aged visibly and his hair actually seemed to whiten. Christopher pitied him and so did everybody else, and by and by public sentiment was almost more concerned with his unhappiness than with the tragedy that caused it.

"Dad doesn't harbor any grudge against you, Mr. Hollings!" repeated the lad for the twentieth time, in a hope of consoling the unfortunate clerk. "Neither does Mr. Norcross. I heard him tell my father so."

"That isn't the point, sonny," his listener responded dejectedly. "Of course it's kind of them not to blame me. They'd be well within their rights were they to turn me off. What bothers me is that I should let such a thing happen."

"You couldn't help it."

"I know—I know. It doesn't seem as if I could," the man answered, shaking his head. "But I ought to have helped it—somehow."

That was Hollings' constant lament.

Round and round in a circle went he and Christopher, the lad constantly trying to brighten and encourage, and the clerk as invariably bringing up with this same doleful plaint. He was not to be comforted.

In the meantime Christopher, along with offering optimistic and repeated assertions that the diamonds would surely be found, was gleaning a surprising amount of information as he flitted about the store. He learned not only of clocks but interesting bits concerning the value and cutting of gems, the repairing of jewelry; the patterns of silverware, strange facts about pearls.

Since he was free to browse wherever he chose, he found no monotony in his environment. Furthermore he gradually sifted out the men who had made something of their calling and attached himself to them because they invariably proved to be the most interesting. Those who merely sold what they had to sell and received the money he classed as bores and thereafter avoided.

It was amazing how many more of the latter there were than the former. The man possessing a broad knowledge of the wares he handled was rare. Several clerks, for example, were behind the gem counters but the boy soon discovered that when they wished an expert opinion they with one accord turned to a stumpy little fellow with a bald head who appeared to know every stone in the showcase by heart and knew just what country it came from; whether it was well cut; if it was perfect or marred by flaws; whether it was a tinge off the desired color, and numerous other facts concerning it. Christopher had not dreamed there was so much to know about precious stones, let alone all the wealth of romance connected with them as Mr. Rhinehart had stored up.

He could tell you where were the largest diamonds, rubies, and emeralds in the world; who owned them, and what they were worth; could give the history of many of the finest pearls and celebrated necklaces made from them; and at his tongue's end were stories regarding various gems as thrilling and delightful as any Arabian Night's tales. He it was who also had not only read about but had actually seen many of the crown jewels of the world and knew where celebrated collections of cameos, jade, and quaint Egyptian ornaments were exhibited. Indeed he seemed to have read and studied omnivorously and not a week passed that he did not add to his store of learning some interesting romance of a pair of old Sheffield candlesticks or a royal ruby.

In fact Mr. Rhinehart was not just a man; he was a walking story-book, and, like McPhearson, a thoroughly delightful companion. Oh, he did not consider his job a humdrum one, it was easy to see that. He had lifted the traffic of jeweled ornaments, by means of which he earned his daily bread, out of the class of mere salesmanship.

"You never get tired of your work, do you, Mr. Rhinehart?" commented Christopher, when on a day trade was light, he stood listening to the alluring adventure of a string of black pearls.

"Tired of it? Why should I?"

"But lots of the men do," was the naïve observation. "They come in yawning in the morning, and seem bored to death at having to do the same old thing."

Mr. Rhinehart smiled.

"Work is what you make of it. A job can be interesting and carry you far beyond its narrow limitations or it can sink into becoming a daily grind. It's all as you see it. You get out of it just about what you put in."

"I begin to think you do," agreed Christopher. "I'm sure Mr. McPhearson, who repairs clocks upstairs, gets a hundred times more fun out of them than do the other men."

"McPhearson, the old Scotchman, you mean? A fine old chap, isn't he? So you have picked him out already! Well, you have chosen well, for there is almost nothing about clocks that he doesn't know," asserted Mr. Rhinehart with enthusiasm.

"I had no idea there was so much to know about them," confided the boy. "All I ever thought about a clock was to look and see whether it was right or not, and blame it if it wasn't. Now I've begun to believe it is pretty wonderful when it is."

"It is pretty wonderful," Mr. Rhinehart agreed. "The trouble with us is that we live in an age of wonders and have come to accept with complacency the fruit of the many brains that have given us myriads of perfect mechanisms. Almost every convenience and luxury about us was produced by toil and patient experiment. Clocks, for example, were very long in becoming the fine, reliable products they now are, as no doubt you have already learned. When their first makers got them to go at all the feat seemed so remarkable that the fact they did not keep good time was entirely lost sight of. But just you let *our* clocks or watches vary a minute or two a week, and we are quite out of humor with them, never taking into consideration how we jolt them about and subject them to heat, cold, and irregular winding. Where can you find any other piece of machinery that will run as long or as faithfully with so little care?

"A drop or two of oil, a cleaning now and then, and on they go without whimper or complaint, always ticking cheerfully. And the only thanks they ever receive is to be scolded at when they fail to any small degree." Mr. Rhinehart paused, then added drily, "Did any of us human machines do our work as well, we should have earned the right to belabor them. As it is I consider we stand on rather delicate ground when we berate either a clock or a watch—especially an old one."

"Mr. McPhearson is fixing now a bracket clock made about 1720."

"He is? That means it has ticked and ticked over two hundred years, doesn't it! Neither your machinery nor mine will last that long. Think of the changes a veteran like that has outlived. It would be interesting, wouldn't it, if it could recount its history and tell us where it has been all that long time? A clock that survives for such a stretch of years is lucky, for it must have changed hands many times and traveled far from its birthplace. Moreover, fashion is fickle and owners are seldom loyal enough to respect what is shabby and old. In consequence many a clock has been sentenced to the attic or cellar, there to lie idle and rust out its life. That is the reason a genuine antique clock made by one of the fine makers is so valuable, and why so many of them have disappeared. There are types that are scarce as hen's teeth. Their owners, carried away by more modern designs, could not get them to the junkman fast enough."

Christopher would have laughed at Mr. Rhinehart's indignation had it not been so genuine.

"Oh, I won't pretend some of the more recent products may not be better than some of those of the past. Nevertheless an old clock, every part of which was carefully fashioned by the hand of an intelligent maker in deliberate, painstaking manner, is a far finer product than most of those turned out by poor machinery. For you know—or will learn—that there are clocks *and clocks*. Many firms make them but all do not excel. Therefore I would counsel those who own the old aristocrats produced by skilled makers to hold on to them, even if they venerate neither their history nor their age. They may discard a treasure they cannot equal or replace. On the face of it, it stands to reason that any mechanism which will run two centuries or more was turned out by a workman who knew what he was about."

"That's what Mr. McPhearson thinks," said Christopher, rising. "Clocks are almost people to him."

"Are you going, sonny?"

"Yes, I guess I'll quit bothering you and bother Mr. McP-hearson for a while. Dad said I mustn't make too long calls on people."

Moving off, the lad called the elevator and ascended to the fourth floor where he found his friend, the Scotchman, in the lowest of spirits.

"Well, she's gone!" exclaimed he mournfully. "I couldn't in conscience keep her here any longer when she was running so well."

"The bracket clock, you mean?"

"I do. I sent Hammond with her. He should have brains enough to land her at home without jouncing the life out of her; and he ought to be able to put her in place and make sure she is ticking even. If not, I shall have to go up where she lives and make sure for myself."

"You don't often leave the shop, do you?"

"Oh, sometimes. I haven't lately because it hasn't happened to be necessary. Moreover, I have had a good deal to do right here. The fall is my season for trotting about. After houses have been closed all summer and owners have neglected their clocks, I have to go round and start them again. What a barbarous custom it is to let clocks run down and stand idle for months! Why, if asked to do so, we can always send reliable men into houses to wind the clocks and keep them regulated. It costs only a trifle and pays in the end, if people were only aware of it. A clock neither wants nor needs a rest. On the contrary it is never so happy as when it is ticking. The woman who stopped her clock nights so it should not be wearing out the works did it no kindness."

A peal of appreciative laughter came from Christopher.

McPhearson reached for a small traveling clock and unscrewed the back of it.

"Humph!" sniffed he. "Solid with dirt! I'll wager it hasn't been cleaned for years. Still, it is expected to go all the same. If its owner had half that amount of dust in his eye he would be off to an oculist as fast as ever his feet would carry him. Such creatures do not deserve to have clocks. They should have lived when there weren't any."

"Back in the thirteenth century, you mean?" queried Christopher, not unwilling to display his knowledge.

"Oh, they were just beginning to get them by that time," McPhearson objected instantly. "By the fourteenth century there were clocks that really began to be clocks. In 1326, for example, the Abbott of St. Albans made a marvelous clock which not only showed the course of the sun and moon but the ebb and flow of the tide. In the meantime more big clocks began to be put up on the church towers. But remember, none of these could boast any nice degree of accuracy; it was many, many years later before the secrets of correct time-keeping were mastered. Nevertheless every little while a leap forward would be made, and one of these jumps came about 1340 when Peter Lightfoot, a monk, made for Glastonbury Abbey a clock with an escapement and regulator for securing equitable motion."

Christopher, passing over the latter facts, seized upon the former.

"Another monk!" cried he.

The Scotchman nodded.

"I told you it was the monks who packed their time the fullest and paid the greatest heed to the hours in those days."

The boy did not answer immediately and when he did it was to venture politely:

"I suppose *equitable motion* was a fine thing."

McPhearson peeped at him over the top of his glasses.

"Have you any idea, laddie, what it was?" he interrogated.

"Not the remotest," came frankly from Christopher.

They both laughed.

"Well, what I am talking about is our dead beat escapement."

"And what might that be?"

McPhearson became thoughtful.

"Well, there are various methods of reaching the desired result, the chief aim of which is that at the end of each swing of the pendulum the escape teeth shall be made to stop until the pendulum starts to swing back again. This can be achieved by beveling both tooth and pallet until the teeth, instead of recoiling by the downward motion of the pallet, shall slip by and give the pallet a jolt onward, thereby keeping it in motion. Look here, and I'll show you what I mean. Even this small clock has an escapement that works after that plan."

The boy rose and peered into the mysterious works of the clock.

"Oh, I see now," he exclaimed. "That would help to make the beat more even, wouldn't it, and insure better time? And now what about Peter Lightfoot's clock? Of course it isn't in existence now?"

"That clock had quite a history, son," was the old man's reply. "When the Reformation came and there was danger of its being destroyed, it was moved to Wells Cathedral, and there a part, at least, of the original structure still remains. In 1835, however, its works were found to be pretty well worn out (scant wonder, too) and therefore new works were put in and the dial was repaired. Evidently, long before, the clock had had at its base some revolving horseman which probably delighted the people of that time who were always pleased by automatic figures and scenes in pantomime. Many ancient clocks reflected this childish taste by having attached to them all sorts of figures representing the hours, days of the week, or feasts of the Church. Probably one reason for this was that as the education of the populace was too meager to give them much knowledge of numerals, and as they had but little business of importance to transact, they were far less interested in the time than in the dumb show gone through with by the little carved dolls. Furthermore, having no calendars, these figures served the purpose of telling them what day it was and reminding them of the church holidays. This explains why so many of the early clockmakers devoted such a degree of energy and skill to fashioning all sorts of pantomimes to be enacted by miniature figures at certain hours.

"There was the Exeter clock, for instance, which Jacob Lovelace took thirty-four years to make, and which had thirteen different mechanisms. It did no end of ingenious things. Figures passed in procession at the arrival of the hour; tiny bell ringers rang miniature chimes. In fact, so many things went on that to see it was almost as good as a play. No wonder that when Jacob Lovelace died in 1716 it was called his masterpiece."

"Wasn't there some sort of wonderful clock at Venice?" Christopher asked timidly.

"Yes, indeed! There was a very celebrated seventeenth century clock there, with a blue and gold dial which had above it bronze figures that struck the hour on a bell. Moreover, when the noon of Ascension Day came, the people were reminded of this holy feast by seeing the Magi issue forth from a little door and how before the Virgin, who held in her arms the Christ Child. Every noontime for two weeks this scene was enacted, to the vast delight of a simple, childish people. This is the reason why most clocks of the period had only an hour hand and stressed events of the calendar rather than pointing the flight of the minutes."

"It seems funny to think of clocks without minute hands, doesn't it?" Christopher mused.

"Not so funny when you consider what life was at that time and how poorly equipped the public was in arithmetic. Many of them knew nothing of hours or quarter hours. But when the chimes in the village church played a different tune each day of the week—a tune they knew—they soon came to understand, for example, that the Blue Bells of Scotland meant Tuesday, and that Annie Laurie, perhaps, meant Thursday."

"You do get horribly mixed on the days of the week when you have no calendar and nothing especial to do," asserted Christopher quickly. "I remember once when I was in the Maine woods with dad, we both got so confused we hadn't a notion what day it was."

"Ah, then you have some understanding of the dilemma of your long-ago ancestors," smiled McPhearson, "and can comprehend why they were so thankful to have the cathedral clock set them right. Noblemen who owned outlying castles would send their servants to the village square, not only to find out the hour but to learn of the sun, moon, stars, and the religious feasts and fasts. For, you see, the majority of the clocks were put up by the clergy for the purpose not only of regulating their own monastic life, but to prod worshipers to remember the masses and prescribed feasts of the abbeys.

"Later on when clocks and watches came into more general use, and the making of them was done by artisans instead of monks, time-keeping passed out of the hands of the Church (just as the printing of books did later on) and into the hands of guild members and manufacturers. It was when this change became effective that the character of clocks shifted very materially. The religious figures disappeared together with the elaborate pantomimes that accompanied them, and the clockmakers directed their energies to making the clock primarily a time-telling agency. However, all that was not accomplished in a minute, and when you go abroad, as you will some day, and see some of the quaint old clocks with their procession of Biblical figures, just remember how it was they happened to be made, and what interesting curiosities they are."

"I'm afraid by the time I ever get to Europe there won't be any such clocks to be seen," sighed Christopher.

"Oh, yes, there will! You will see, for example, the great clock of Straasburg. Not, to be sure, the original one, for that was made in 1352; neither will you view its successor put up in the latter part of the sixteenth century. Both of those have long since disappeared. Still the third one, which succeeded them and is now well on to a hundred years old, is wonderful enough to excite your admiration. It was inaugurated October 2, 1842, and is one of the marvels of the Old World. Certainly it incidentally provides the people with all they could ask in the way of information and entertainment. On a level with the ground is a globe telling of the stars visible to the naked eye—their rising, setting, and passage over the meridian. Behind this is a calendar indicating the year, month, and day, together with all ecclesiastical feasts and holidays. Above these two is a gallery where allegorical figures passing from left to right symbolize the days of the week.

"Apollo, drawn in his chariot by prancing horses, typifies Sunday; Monday we have Diana with her stag. Tuesday comes Mars, Wednesday Mercury, Thursday Jupiter, Friday we have the goddess Venus, and Saturday Saturn."

"Some clock!" gasped Christopher.

"Oh, that isn't half of it," protested McPhearson, "although it sounds amazing enough; there is yet more. Above all these gods and goddesses is a clock dial showing ordinary time; a contrivance that gives the movements of the planets; and a globe indicating the phases of the moon. Nor have we reached the end of the marvels yet. Still higher up are figures to symbolize childhood, youth, manhood, and old age, each of which strikes one of the quarter hours. Beside the ordinary clock dial you will see a moving figure that strikes with its scepter the first note of each quarter hour, while at the same time a figure opposite it turns an hourglass to mark the complete passing of the hour."

"Gee!"

"Oh, don't imagine you are through with this marvelous clock yet. There is in addition a grim statuette of death which is to remind man of his frailty and the shortness of his days;

this strikes each hour with a bone. It is at the very top that we get the touch of more modern Christianity in a procession of the twelve apostles, who at noon pass before a figure of Christ, bowing at his feet, while he makes the sign of the cross in response, and it is at this instant that the tragic denial of Peter is portrayed by a cock, which from its perch on one of the turrets, flaps its wings and crows three times."

"Why, it would almost be worth a trip to Europe to see such a wonder!" burst out Christopher.

"Almost. You could also see the clock at Berne while you were about it—a clever mechanism made by the Swiss in 1527. Berne, as you doubtless know, if you have faithfully studied your geography, took its name from the word *bären*, meaning bears; and you know, too, how it came about that the Swiss selected that name for it. In all the shops you will find large and small bears for sale, all carved from wood and converted to every imaginable purpose."

"And the clock—has it bears too?"

"It certainly has. Three minutes before the hour a cock gives warning of the time by crowing and flapping its carved wings. Then out comes a procession of bears that march solemnly round a bearded Father Time, whereupon the cock crows again, and a jester, hammer in hand, strikes a bell. At the sound the bearded old man raises his sceptre, opens his mouth, and turns an hourglass. And at each stroke of the bell a bear nods his head. All this done, the cock crows again and the fantastic pantomime is finished.

"You therefore can see how it came about that when the nobles and the rich began to wish to have clocks of their own, in order to save the trouble of sending their servants to the public square to find out all the big clocks had to tell, clockmakers felt they must give them at least some of the things to which they had become accustomed, and therefore made clocks showing the sun, moon, stars, or tides, or those that would play tunes on miniature chimes of six or eight bells. It was all a relic of the past. Possibly, too, clockmakers were curious to see what they could do in more limited space. Be this as it may, musical clocks died hard. The old bracket clock we have just sent home, you will recall, played seven different tunes. Purchasers liked the notion of having music to mark the hours. Later on, however, when they became better educated, the frivolous little tinkling jigs and dances gave place to a more dignified and sonorous striking of a single rich-toned bell, or a group of such bells, and resulted in the Westminster chimes or others not unlike them."

"The little tunes were mighty jolly though," observed Christopher, with evident regret.

"Very jolly indeed. Nevertheless one tired of them sooner than of the graver notes. I think I told you how, when Richard Parsons' clock made its first appearance here in the shop, everybody within hearing distance dropped his work and came running to listen to its music. The men were eager as children. For days they watched the time so to be sure not to miss nine, twelve, and three o'clock. Then the novelty wore off, and the audience gradually diminished."

"I should never be tired of listening," Christopher announced.

"Nor I. Perhaps, though, that is because the quaintness of the themes appeals to us more than does the tone of the bells themselves, for their cadence is, you must admit, a bit thin and suggestive of a music box."

"Maybe. But I like music boxes."

"In that case, Richard Parsons' music cannot fail to please you. Who knows but you may be owning one of these bracket clocks of your own some day? You better begin to save up your pennies."

"It would take too many, I'm afraid."

"I grant that it would take quite a few."

CHAPTER VII

AN EXCURSION

NOTHER week passed and still no tidings of the stolen diamonds came. The inspector, to be sure, asserted with high confidence that he had clews but apparently they were tangled tracks reaching too far away to bring immediate results; neither would he confide what they were. Instead he shook his head sagely, cautioned patience, and merely observed he was giving the culprits plenty of rope.

This information was disheartening enough to Mr. Burton, his partner, and Christopher himself, but to the unfortunate Hollings it was well-nigh exasperating.

"Anybody'd think we had half a century to land those thieves," snarled he. "Why, they have had almost time enough to get to Holland or Siam, and dispose of their loot. I can't see what the police are thinking of not to round them up quicker than this. Since they have a description of the men and can even call them by names there is no excuse for them—none."

"My father seems to think the men at headquarters know what they are about," Christopher said, making an attempt to soothe the ire of the distressed clerk.

"Maybe they do," sighed Hollings. "I hope so." Nevertheless, there was no spontaneity in his optimism.

Thus the days went along and Christopher came to find in

them great contentment. Perhaps his serenity was due in part to the fact that the weakness of his eyes shut him out so completely from almost every other diversion that he welcomed any sort of companionship with disproportionate appreciation. He could not read, he could not write, he could go neither to the theater nor the movies. And while he thus halted and marked time, the world and everybody in it marched along without giving him a thought. What marvel, therefore, that he attached himself eagerly to any person who was kind and willing to bother with him?

It had not taken him long to sift out those who tolerated him from motives of pity or policy and those who really liked him, and he was not a little proud to class in the latter group both Mr. Rhinehart and the Scotchman, McPhearson. Mr. Rhinehart not only had boys of his own but was in addition enough of a boy himself to be dowered with a keen sympathy and understanding of them.

McPhearson, on the other hand, was a solitary creature whose forlornity prompted him to take with gladness any hand stretched out to him. He lived alone in dingy bachelor quarters, where, save for his books and his flute, he had few companions. Therefore he came to look forward to Christopher's daily visits with an even greater degree of anticipation than did the lad himself.

"I've got to go out to-day," was his greeting when Christopher made his appearance on a cold December morning.

The boy's face fell.

"What do you say to coming with me? Would your father be willing?"

"Oh, he wouldn't care. Where are you going?"

"Out to Morningside Drive to look at a clock that they want me to see."

"When are you leaving?"

"Right away. I was waiting a second or two to see if you'd put in an appearance."

"That was awfully good of you. I'll get my coat."

"You'd better ask your father."

"Don't worry. He'll think it's all right."

"Still, I'd rather you asked him."

"If it will make you any easier in your mind, I will. It won't take a second."

Off rushed Christopher, only to return breathless a moment or two later.

"Dad says I can go as long as it's with you. And he told me to tell you we needn't rush the trip. Here's money for our fares."

Christopher extended a fresh new bill.

"Pooh! Pooh! Nonsense!" growled McPhearson. "We'll not need that. I've money enough. Besides, we're only going in the bus."

"No matter. Dad said—"

"Come along," interrupted the Scotchman, catching up his bag of tools and cutting short further discussion. "If we stand here arguing we shall never get off at all."

Docilely Christopher followed him into the street where amid surging crowds they hailed the bus and began rolling up the avenue.

"New York couldn't get along very well without clocks, could it?" commented Christopher, as he looked down upon the maelstrom of hurrying humanity.

"Not very well," laughed his companion. "I suppose the majority of this rushing mob is aiming to arrive somewhere at a specified time. There are probably men with business engagements; women with dressmakers' and dentists' appointments;

students hastening to lectures; people going for trains and cars. You may be reasonably certain it is the clock that is spurring them forward. Earlier in the day the throngs would have been denser than this, for then we should have seen the workers who pour into the city every morning. As it is there are quite enough of them. So it goes from dawn until dusk. Everybody moves on schedule and it is precisely because the day is cut up into this checkerboard of hours that we can fit our work and play together and accomplish so much in it."

"It doesn't leave us much time for play," suggested Christopher mischievously.

"No, I am afraid it doesn't—not enough time. Somehow the proportions have become distorted. We consider play almost a waste of time and with life short as it is, to fool time away has become little short of a sin. Certainly to waste another person's time is criminal—the actual stealing of a valuable commodity that can never be replaced."

"People who are late never seem to consider themselves thieves," grinned Christopher.

"They ought to," McPhearson answered solemnly. "Everybody's time has a money equivalent in these days. If a man keeps me waiting or talks my time away, he robs me of five or ten or twenty dollars, according to the length of the interval he has kept me from my work."

"Great Scot!" exclaimed the boy in consternation. "At that rate I've run up a whale of a bill."

McPhearson laughed at the ejaculation.

"Cheer up, son! I shall not attack your bank account yet," said he. "You see, when I talk to you I can work at the same time, which puts quite a different phase on the matter; and when I cannot both work and talk, why I stop talking. But if I were with some one else it might be my work that would have to stop, and my talk go on, and that would make all the difference.”

“Sure!”

“It is useless for us to kick against the rush of the age in which we live,” continued McPhearson. “We are here and must move with the tide. But if we had been born a few hundred years ago, one day would have been so like another that to waste moments or even hours would not have greatly mattered. In fact, people expected to waste time and wait about for nearly everything they wanted. Clothing was made by hand and it took a long time to make it. Even the cloth was spun at home after the day's work was finished, and there was nothing else to do. When you traveled, roads were poor and the stage-coaches obliged to halt at intervals for fresh horses. In the meantime you stopped at an inn and hung about, waiting not only for your own dinner but until the drivers and horses had had theirs. Afterward more precious moments were consumed in harnessing up the new steeds and getting once more under way. Then if no wheels came off, or reins broke, or horses stumbled, not to mention possible onslaughts of highwaymen who beset unfrequented districts, you eventually arrived at your destination.”

“At that rate I should never expect to get anywhere,” announced Christopher.

“All living proceeded at that ratio or even a slower one, for if you could not afford coach fare you *walked* to where you were going. Nevertheless, in spite of the defects of the period, it was considered a very comfortable era, and people were well content with it. Fortunately nobody wished to travel very extensively, for as knowledge of geography was scant they did not know there was anywhere to go. Hence they cheerfully remained in the spot where they happened to be born or within a short radius of it.

"About the great estates hung swarms of retainers who in times of peace had little to do. Some of these helped dress the venison brought in from the hunt, some dragged in logs for the fires, some cared for the horses; and with all that there were several times as many retainers as there were duties. Therefore it was unavoidable that many men were idle the greater part of the day. Indeed they had not resources enough to be anything else, for scarce a one of them had any education. They could neither read nor write, and in many cases, their masters could do no better. The bare fact that a nobleman sent his servant to the public square to find out what time it was proves that such little things as quarter or half hours did not concern them much.

"Ladies worked tapestries, danced and sang their days away; gossiped with one another or quarreled with their maids, while the gentlemen of the household hunted, hung about the court, loitered at the inn or rowed on the river. For such an existence as that one did not need to slice his time up into very fine pieces. An idle, leisurely life it was, with little cause for haste. What wonder the clocks had no minute hands when even hours were of such minor importance?"

The bus halted with a jerk, to escape running over an abnormally daring pedestrian.

"A second made some difference to him," said Christopher, when once more the vehicle was in motion.

"All the difference between being in this world and out of it," was the terse reply. "He'd better have lost a minute rather than take a chance like that. But, alas, we have got into the habit of thinking we cannot stop for anything. From morning to night we race about as if the bogey man were at our heels. Sometimes I wish myself in the forest of Arden, where there were no clocks."

"You'd have nothing to repair there, certainly."

"I know it. And before a week was out I should be the most miserable of mortals, in consequence," retorted the Scotchman quickly. "No, no! It is better to be perched up here on a bus whizzing to doctor a balky old clock than to be idle day in and day out."

"Where is the balky old clock you mention?" Christopher inquired.

"In a fine mansion not far from here," replied McPhearson. "A rich old gentleman who is a clock collector lives there all alone with enough servants to man a warship. You may be sure our shoe leather will not be wasted, for none of his clocks are ever out of commission because of neglect or foolish handling."

Signaling the bus, the travelers descended into the street and walked a few blocks.

"You are sure your old gentleman won't mind my coming with you?" murmured Christopher, as they neared the house.

"Oh, Mr. Hawley won't mind. I have been coming here for years. He never lets anybody else touch his clocks. If he is at home, he will probably be proud as a peacock to show you his treasures; and if he isn't you can look about by yourself. He never minds what I do."

On investigation, however, it proved that Mr. Hawley was not at home.

"He done gone to some board meeting this morning," explained the colored butler. "And sorry enough he'll be to miss you too, Mr. McPhearson, for he always likes havin' a talk with you."

"Which clock is it this time, Ebenezer?"

"Number Seventeen, sir," answered the man gravely. "She done been kickin' up something vexatious. She absumlutely won't strike with the others—absumlutely won't! After the rest of 'em are through, in she comes a minute late, chiming away on her own hook, all independent like, as if she was runnin' the world. You know what that means. Mr. Hawley, sir, he won't stand for no nonsense like that—not for a second. If there's any strikin' to be done round here, or chimin' either, it's got to be done in chorus or not at all. Ain't he been well-nigh a year trainin' those clocks? We've got 'em down now almighty fine too—'cept for Number Seventeen."

"I'll have a look at her."

"Do, sir! She's on the stairway, you know, halfway up."

"Oh, I remember her, although I don't believe I could give her number offhand."

"I could. I could recite the numbers of them clocks frontways an' backways," answered Ebenezer. "You could, too, if you had 'em to wind."

"Oh, you wind them now, do you?"

"I certainly do!" affirmed the negro, with no small degree of pride. "Mr. Hawley's been a long time comin' to it, but at last he's let me. Yes, sir! I wind 'em, every one."

"Indeed!"

"Yes. You see, Mr. Hawley ain't so young as he was, an' mor'n that, he's got rheumatism in his arm. So one mornin' he say to me 'Ebenezer,' he say, 'I reckon you'll have to take on the windin' up. My hand is gettin' shaky.' Well, sir, had he given me the management of a railroad I couldn't have been prouder. That's why, when Seventeen begun branchin' out for herself, I was so 'specially upset. I wondered what I'd done to her."

"We'll look and see," McPhearson smiled. "Very likely she's just taken a whim, Ebenezer."

"I hope so—I do indeed, sir."

Following the old butler, Christopher and the Scotchman ascended the stairs until they came to a niche where stood the clock in question.

It was perhaps four feet tall—an exact replica of a long-case clock.

"I never saw such a little grandfather's clock as that," commented Christopher.

"It is a bracelet clock of early Colonial make," McPhearson explained. "Many of them were made in Massachusetts in the early days."

"And its works are like the big ones?"

"Practically, yes. This one, as you see, was made by John Bailey of Hanover, a small town on Cape Cod. Probably its date is about 1812 or 1815."

"It is over a hundred years old already."

"Yes. And considering it is, don't you think, Ebenezer, it has earned the right to a little independence?" McPhearson inquired of the man, a twinkle in his eye.

But Ebenezer shook his head.

"Mr. Hawley done say no clock can go strikin' by herself—no matter how old she is," Ebenezer asserted, without hint of a smile. "He say there's no excuse for it—no excuse!"

McPhearson opened the door and glanced inside.

"Can you see anything wrong, sir?" queried the old butler eagerly.

"Not yet. I've got to make a more thorough examination."

"Likely you have. But whatever's the matter, you'll find it—I know that. I never see such a man for clocks as you in all my born days; an' the master, he say the same. 'Mr. McPhearson will soon get Seventeen into line,' he says, an' I know you will, sir. Don't you always?"

In the meantime Christopher had peeped inside the clock.

"Why, look at the great lead weight!" ejaculated he.

"Yes. Many old clocks had weights such as this, which were pulled up when the clock was wound and gradually dropped as the clock ran down. Sometimes a stone was used; sometimes even a pail of small stones."

"But where were springs and pendulums?" gasped the astonished boy.

"Springs came a good deal later. Even pendulums were not introduced in any practical form until 1657. Up to that time a balance did the work. The advent of the pendulum, invented probably by Christian Huygens, a Dutch mathematician, opened up no end of complications for the early clockmakers. In the first place they could not decide where to put this new article. Some placed the pendulum at the front of their clock, letting it dangle down across the face; others tried to conceal it by hanging it outside the back. Still others made a dial that would project enough at either side to cover it up.

"Nor did the novel innovation of the pendulum do much good at first, although theoretically makers of clocks conceded pendulums to be a scientific advance over older methods. Of course the theory of the pendulum had been for a long time in the minds of many thoughtful persons. Galileo had seized on its principle when observing the swinging of lanterns in the church at Pisa, and had written a scientific treatise on it. But to get an idea is one thing and to apply it is quite another. Pendulums were very complicated mechanisms. In the first place the length of the pendulum decides, you see, the rate of the clock's vibration; a short one resulting in a quick, nervous tick; and a long one in a slow, quiet one. Therefore pendulums meant more even vibration and more accurate time-keeping, and it was just when makers were rejoicing over these advantages that it was discovered the temperature of the place in which a clock stood affected the rod the bob hung on and threw the whole timepiece out of adjustment. Here was a pretty kettle of fish! A hot room, for example, would expand the rod and lengthen it."

"And make the clock tick slower," put in Christopher eagerly.

"Precisely."

"Then the clock would go slower sometimes than others."

"Exactly that! The variation was not great, of course, and we now have learned how to meet it by lengthening or shortening the pendulum by means of a screw placed near the bob. Nevertheless the variation is there. A common wire pendulum will vary approximately a minute a week; a brass rod will, on the other hand, vary that same minute in five days instead of seven. Wood, a material showing less change than metal, will vary only a minute in three weeks.

"All this we have learned to make allowance for. But the poor old clockmakers had to gather these facts by long and tiresome experiment. At length brass pendulums which, they discovered, made the most trouble, were replaced by those of iron or lead which, being of softer material, expanded and contracted more readily. In our day you will sometimes see a very finely adjusted astronomical clock whose pendulum terminates in a hollow glass or iron receptacle filled with mercury, instead of the usual metal bob."

"There are two of them at the store."

"To be sure there are! For the moment I had forgotten that."

"And all this time while clockmakers were fussing round about bobs and pendulums, did the people have to keep on running to the cathedral or the public square to find out what time it was?"

"No, indeed! By 1600 you could buy for a moderate sum a clock to use at home. Not that it was a very accurate timekeeper. Nevertheless it gave a fair idea of the hour, which was all that was demanded of it," laughed McPhearson, busying himself with his screwdriver.

"What sort of clocks were the first ones?"

"They were not like ours, you must remember that. There was, for instance, the bird-case clock, a small chased or perforated brass affair from four to five inches square, and named because its shape suggested a cage for birds. I spoke of it before. Then there was the lantern clock. Both these varieties were made to hang on the wall and were wound by pulling down the weights that dangled from them."

"They had no springs, pendulums or things?" questioned Christopher wonderingly.

"That was before the days of springs. This particular type of clock, however, had a pendulum; but it was only a pendulum driven by weights showing the pendulum idea in its crudest form. Not until the long-case (or grandfather) clock made its advent into England did the pendulum, scientifically applied, come into being; and before that era many years intervened during which bracket clocks held the center of the stage."

"Clocks like Richard Parsons'!" interrupted Christopher triumphantly.

"Yes, the very same. These were better yet because they had no weights hanging down and so could be put on a table, a shelf, or mantelpiece. In the meantime, somewhere about the year 1500, a Nurenburg locksmith named Peter Henlien had made a clock so small that it could be carried in one's pocket—if that pocket was of pretty ample size. It had works of iron, one hand, and no crystal, and was, to be sure, both thick and clumsy, but it boasted one amazing feature. Since it was too small to depend on weights, it contained a coiled mainspring—something entirely new to the clockmaking world. Now this article fashioned by Peter Henlien cannot be termed a watch as we know watches; but still it was the nearest approach to one that had yet been produced. The fact that this egg-shaped concoction was no great timekeeper was a secondary matter. The important thing was that a small, compact article that would keep some sort of time had been made, and a coiled mainspring was inside it."

"How funny to have a blacksmith—or rather a locksmith, making a watch!"

"Not at all. Records show that a great many of the best clockmakers belonging to the Clockmakers' Company were, or had formerly been, blacksmiths."

"But it seems odd, doesn't it?" mused Christopher. "And did everybody start making watches after this queer article of Peter Henlien's was produced?"

"Not very extensively. Indeed, there was nothing very appealing or attractive in Peter Henlien's watch. Moreover, since such objects failed to keep good time, what earthly inducement was there for owning one? Nevertheless horologers themselves were not discouraged. They kept right on trying to turn out something better, and in 1525 Jacob Zech, a Swiss mechanic from Prague, hit on a remedy to prevent these crude watches from running fast when first wound up and slower when they began to run down. In other words he discovered something that would equalize the mechanism."

"And what was that?"

"A fusee."

"I'm afraid that doesn't help me much," was Christopher's rueful plaint.

"Well, a fusee was a short cone having a spiral groove round it, with a cord or chain wound to the groove and fastened at the big end of the cone. It was a simple device but it did the work. The shaft of the fusee was attached to the large wheel that moved the gears, and the other end of the cord was fastened to the mainspring barrel. Therefore as the mainspring slowly turned the barrel, it gradually uncoiled the cord from the fusee, making it turn and as soon as it turned, the wheels had to turn too, and the watch began to go. Since from the very start the cord unwound from the small end of the cone where the leverage was least, and as the force of the mainspring decreased it, the leverage of the cord strengthened in the same proportion. So you see, the power which turned the wheels was constantly the same. Do not dream, however, this result was reached all in a minute. The crude fusee of Zech had to be perfected by Gruet, another Swiss clockmaker, and by still others. Nevertheless the scheme did work and caused a revolution in clock and watch making. There was now some hope that ultimately timepieces would furnish correct time, which after all is, I suppose, the only excuse a clock has for being."

McPhearson brought from his bag a small copper oil can.

"Wants oilin', does she?" interpolated the butler, who had been standing anxiously near by.

"A drop won't hurt her."

"Much wrong with her, sir?"

"Next to nothing, Ebenezer. She just needed a little readjusting and tightening up."

"Praise de Lord! Then you're most through, sir."

"Pretty near."

"I'm clean afraid Mr. Hawley won't get back before you finish."

"I'm not gone yet."

"Oh, I ain't in any hurry to shoo you out, Mr. McPhearson," declared the man hurriedly. "No, indeed, sir. I could listen to you talk all day."

"I forgot you were listening, Ebenezer."

"Listening? 'Deed an' I was listenin'! My two ears was pricked up like a rabbit's."

The clockmaker flushed and smiled.

"They's silver to clean; an' brasses to polish, an' I dunno what—" continued the butler, "but I'm lettin' 'em all lie 'til by an' by—I's improvin' my mind—I is!"

"So am I," rejoined Christopher, laughing.

"I seem to be furnishing a lecture free of charge to a very select audience," the Scotchman returned drily; "and having once started, I suppose I may as well finish it. You can testify that at least I have not been idle while talking.

"Nor was the era, of which I have been speaking, an idle one. Like Rip Van Winkle, it began slowly to awaken from its long sleep and become alert. Printing was invented and the Bible, along with other books, gradually reached the hands of the common people. In the meantime, Columbus had made his voyage to America and returned with tales of new lands, stimulating in others a spirit of adventure. The recently evolved compass, as well as the fact that larger and more staunch ships were now to be had, lured persons previously shy of the sea to voyages of discovery. On every hand new ideas were coming to light. In the clock world somebody began making screws to replace the primitive little pins and rivets hitherto employed to fasten wheels and dials in place; glass came into more general use, and by 1600 crystals began to be quite generally in evidence; and the appearance of the minute hand gave evidence that the universe was a busier place and short intervals of time becoming of greater worth. But although the sale of clocks increased, watches were not yet in general use. They were too much of a luxury. People therefore consulted their clocks (if they were lucky enough to have them); hied them to the village square if not; or depended upon their sundials of which there were still many in use. Watchmen also went about the streets crying the hours.

"The rich, to be sure, purchased watches, but they bought them more for ornaments than for use. Those who could afford it frequently owned several, wearing them around their necks on chains or ribbons, and displaying a different one to suit either their costume or their fancy."

"But weren't those old egg-shaped watches heavy and ugly?" asked Christopher.

"Oh, by this time watches had got far beyond that original design and had now become monuments to the goldsmith's art, being small and fashioned in every imaginable design. I regret to say that a great portion of the labor went into the cases, which were beautifully made by hand. There were flowers with watches concealed in their centers; baskets of tiny fruits, hearts, animals, death's-heads—every form that was novel or original. Some cases had on their covers miniatures set in jewels; and there were cases of leather studded with decorations in nail heads. In every instance it was the outside of the watch that interested both purchaser and goldsmith—not the inside. Can you wonder, therefore, that the watch deteriorated into being a mere toy and ornament?"

"How could people be so ridiculous!" exclaimed Christopher with scorn.

"It would have been ridiculous had the art of making watches stopped there," McPhearson acquiesced. "But fortunately, if the public was content with such pretty, silly toy affairs, the horologers were not. Patiently they continued the struggle to make timepieces better; and to prove that all this nonsense about pretty watches was not without value, I will tell you that it was while making a white enamel base on which to paint a miniature that some clever person bethought him how nice a watch face of white enamel would be with black figures printed upon it."

"It is never all loss without some gain, is it?" smiled Christopher. "And clocks?"

"Clocks, too, were sharing the general improvement," answered McPhearson. "The old system of the balance with its accompanying weights and chains had passed, and the pendulum, now becoming less of a puzzle, was coming into vogue. Makers had, however, been convinced by this time that pendulums did not look well hanging down across the faces of clocks, and so they now put them at the back, their swingings being frequently concealed by projecting dials. So you see, the world was moving on."

As he concluded this speech, McPhearson took off his working glasses, substituted for them another pair, and began packing up his tools.

"There!" exclaimed he to Ebenezer, "I think you will find Seventeen will do better after this. Don't blame the poor thing. It wasn't her fault."

"I'm glad to hear you say so, sir," returned the butler with a broad smile. "I always did like that clock."

"The others, you say, are all right."

"Mostly, sir. Number Fifteen lagged a little and kept the master botherin' for a while, but she's catchin' up now. I wouldn't dare have you touch her 'cause she's runnin' too close to be disturbed."

"Then I'll go along. Give my respects to Mr. Hawley, Ebenezer."

"I will, sir," and the butler let his visitors out.

CHAPTER VIII

AN ADVENTURE

As they went out to board a returning bus, Christopher remarked regretfully:

"I'd have given a cent to see the rest of those clocks."

"What clocks?" inquired McPhearson with surprise.

"Why, Mr. Hawley's."

The Scotchman halted abruptly in the middle of the sidewalk.

"My goodness!" ejaculated he. "I never thought of it! Why under the sun didn't you speak up, laddie?"

"I didn't like to," replied the boy with diffidence. "I was afraid it might bother somebody."

"Not an atom. On the contrary Ebenezer would have been proud as a peacock to show them off. You could have been wandering round with him while I was fussing over Seventeen as well as not. It's a pity."

So genuine was the regret in the clockmaker's tone that Christopher hastened to add:

"Oh, it's all right, Mr. McPhearson. Please don't think of it again. I oughtn't to have mentioned it. It doesn't really matter, you know."

Still his companion was not satisfied.

"We might go back," suggested he.

"No, no! It will make you late at the store. Maybe you'll be going up there again some other day and can take me along."

WHAT WAS IT THAT RENDERED THE FIGURE SO FAMILIAR?

"I'm afraid not," replied McPhearson, ruefully. "At least I hope not. If Seventeen behaves herself as I expect she will, I shall not be needed. Well! Well! I am sorry. It wasn't very thoughtful of me."

They walked on and hailing a bus climbed aboard it.

The vehicle was crowded and they made their way in with difficulty, jostling aside its closely packed occupants as they entered.

"Lots of these people will be leaving at the next stop," McPhearson remarked. "They always do."

The prediction was true. At the next corner the passengers poured out, leaving the seats only thinly filled.

As Christopher sank into a seat and drew a long breath of relief his eye wandered idly over those sitting near him, and a stranger opposite arrested his attention.

He was a working man shabbily clothed, and wearing a dingy brown ulster and slouch hat. Between his feet was a much worn leather bag which obviously contained tools. His hair was gray and so was the grizzled beard that partially concealed his features. But it was none of these that held the boy's attention. Something in the way the fellow's collar was pulled up and his hat pulled down; something in the gesture with which he moved his hands to turn his paper aroused a vague memory. Fascinated, the lad watched. What was it that rendered the figure so familiar? He had never seen the man before in his life—he was certain of that. And yet, had he? And if so, where? What was the haunting association that held him spellbound and made it impossible for him to remove his gaze from this person whose features were almost entirely screened from view behind the outspread pages of the morning *Herald*?

Christopher looked away. Of course he didn't know the fellow. Why stare at him? But do what he would, back came his gaze to the same brown-ulstered traveler.

Then the bus lurched, stopped suddenly, and he knew! The man had lowered his paper, and as he turned his head to look out, the boy saw on his right cheek, almost concealed by hat and whiskers, a telltale scar.

The shock of the discovery was so great that it was with difficulty Chris checked a cry of surprise. Yes, it was the hero of the ring adventure—there could be no possible doubt of it. And yet, after all, was it? This person's hair was white and his whiskers too; he was shabby and wore spectacles. The lad began to doubt the conclusion to which he had leaped.

It couldn't be Stuart! A diamond robber would not be journeying about in an electric bus in broad daylight. Such a notion was absurd. Probably it was merely a mannerism that had suggested him.

Nevertheless Christopher continued to regard him attentively, studying the white hand with its long, slender fingers. It was a very clean hand for such a poorly dressed individual to boast. It did not look at all in keeping with the clumsy boots, the frayed trousers, the worn ulster, the battered satchel. It did not appear ever to have done a stroke of work in its life.

Suppose the hand was genuine, and the rest only a disguise? Suppose in reality this was Stuart, the criminal for whom both the Chicago and New York police were searching? Oh, it wasn't likely—it could not be likely. Why should a boy of his age hope to track down a thief when agencies such as these had failed? It was preposterous.

Yet, notwithstanding the argument, the doubt would persist. What if, after all, this was Stuart? Yet if it were, what should he do?

If he began to whisper his suspicious to McPhearson, the thief might overhear and, put on his guard, leave the vehicle; and should he call the conductor to his aid, the man would in all probability be unwilling to believe such a tale and refuse to act. Moreover, perhaps he had no authority to do so anyway.

Poor Christopher! His heart beat until it seemed as if the stranger opposite must hear its throbbing and take warning. If only it were possible to alight from the bus without exciting attention, maybe he and McPhearson could get an officer. He sadly wanted somebody's help and advice. The adventure was one he felt to be too big for him to handle alone.

Nevertheless were he even to suggest leaving the car he knew his companion would not only be surprised but would instantly voice aloud his consternation, and then, of course, the man behind the newspaper would hear.

Still, something must be done. The bus was whizzing on down the avenue, and at any moment his prey might take flight.

A mad resolve formed itself in his mind.

"I think we'll have to get out," he said suddenly. "I don't feel well."

McPhearson wheeled on him, amazed.

"What's the matter?"

"My—my—breakfast, I guess. Can you stop the car?"

"Do you mean you want to get out right here?"

"Yes. I'm dizzy. If I can get some air—"

"Not going to faint away, are you?" queried the Scotchman in consternation.

"I—no—I—guess not."

The kind old clockmaker slipped an arm about his shoulders.

"We'll get out at the next stop, sonny. Too bad you feel mean. It's probably the lurching and bumping of this infernal vehicle. You'll be all right when you get outside."

Without attracting anything more than passing notice, they found themselves in the street and saw the bus disappear down the avenue.

"Feel better?" interrogated McPhearson, anxiously.

"I'm all right. There's not a thing the matter with me. The trouble is that the man opposite us was the chap who pinched that ring from Hollings."

"Are you sure?"

"Pretty sure. At any rate, it's worth tipping off headquarters. Where's there a telephone?"

"There's a drug store just across the street, Christopher. But hold on! What do you mean to do?"

The Scotchman's mind was at best a slow-moving machine, and now it appeared to be too stunned to move at all. Sensing that explanation and argument would delay him, Christopher dashed ahead, the clockmaker panting at his heels.

Fortunately he knew the number, for he had talked with the inspector before. Fortunately, too, he had a nickel in his pocket. Therefore he called headquarters, admonishing the operator to make haste.

A second later a reply came singing over the wire.

"Is Mr. Corrigan, the inspector, there?"

"Just gone out."

"Is Davis, his assistant, in?"

"Yes, sir."

"Rush him here. I want to speak to him."

"Who shall I—"

"No matter who. Get him here quick."

There must have been something in the tone that carried a command, for almost immediately a weak, panting voice answered:

"This—is—Davis, sir."

"I'm Christopher Burton, the son of—"

"Yes, sir, I get it."

"I've left at the corner of Fifth Avenue and West Fifty-seventh Street a bus numbered 1079 that's on its way down town; in it was a man that looked like Stuart. Know who I mean?"

"Jove! You bet I do! Well?"

"He was togged out in an old brown ulster, worn trousers, and boots that were all splashed with plaster or paint, and he had white hair, a white beard, a slouch hat, and a bag. It may not be he at all, you know; but his hands—say—hello—hello—Davis—hello—the darn operator's cut me off."

"Maybe not. More likely Davis hung up the 'phone."

"But I wasn't through," declared the boy indignantly.

"He'd got all he wanted, I imagine, and had to get to work."

"Perhaps so." Christopher, however, was not satisfied.

Moreover, now that the excitement of the incident was over and he began to look back on what he had done, it seemed madness. What right had he to turn the whole police force of the city of New York loose on a poor old working man, solely because his hands happened to be white! It was audacious. A pretty kind of a fool he'd feel if he had started them off on a false scent! They would not thank him. He had fumbled the affair from the beginning, and doubtless was continuing to fumble it.

All the elation died in his face, and noticing this, McPhearson, who loitered in the meantime at the door of the telephone booth, remarked:

"What's the trouble, son?"

"If I was only *sure* it was Stuart."

"That's what I was trying to tell you, laddie, when you ran pell-mell in here to call the police. You ought to have made sure before you gave the information."

"But how could I?" retorted Christopher irritably. "I couldn't go up to the man and ask him politely whether he was the burglar who took a diamond ring from my father's shop, could I?"

The absurdity of the question brought back his good humor.

"No. I grant that," McPhearson agreed. "Still you might have proceeded with a grain less speed. I always think an action can bear considering."

"But all actions can't be considered," was the crisp reply. Again an edge of sharpness had crept into the lad's voice.

"Well, well. Maybe no harm's done," the clockmaker hastened to say soothingly. "No doubt the police chase about on a hundred false clews a day. Their information can't always be right."

"You feel like a fool, though, if you give them the wrong clew."

"Yes, you do."

The promptness of the concession was anything but comforting. Obviously McPhearson felt that in the present instance, at least, the tip offered had been both valueless and absurd. A strained silence fell between them.

"I suppose we may as well hail another bus and get back to the store," the clock repairer at length suggested. "There's no good hanging round here."

Although he did not actually say in so many words that they had already wasted two fares, Christopher, well aware of his Scotch thrift, felt his manner implied it.

They did not say much during the ride down town. McPhearson was a bit ruffled and annoyed, and Christopher crestfallen and mortified. He was thinking, too, that he would have to confess to his father what he had so impulsively done, and receive from him more jeers and ridicule linked with probable admonitions to greater deliberation and caution in future. He hated to be preached at. Therefore he was entirely unprepared for the ovation that greeted his return to the shop.

Hollings was near the door when he went in and had evidently been waiting for him.

"Birdie is securely in his cage!" announced he, dropping his voice so that the thrilling tidings might not be overheard by customers close at hand.

"What?" gasped Christopher.

"Yes, he's bagged for fair! Your father is delighted. They're all upstairs waiting for you—Corrigan, Davis, and all. We're to go down to headquarters and identify the chap."

"Then it really *was* Stuart!"

"Sure thing!" Hollings was actually trembling with joy. "Oh, I hope they'll find those diamonds on him! At least, they'll probably be able to make him tell where they are. If we can only get that ring back, I shall die happy."

"So you were right after all, Christopher," McPhearson put in.

"Apparently!"

The cry, *"I told you so!"* rose like a wave to the lad's lips and then as speedily receded. Why should he feel triumphant? Mistakes are always possible, and he might have been mistaken. Fortunately this time he had not been, that was all.

"I'm glad!" the clockmaker declared.

"So am I!" replied the boy modestly.

No further comment was made except as they went up in the elevator, the old man added:

"It's never amiss to have your eyes about you, son. The majority of folks might as well have two glass beads in their heads, so little do they really observe of what they see. To have your eyes open and your mouth shut isn't a bad notion."

It was like McPhearson to turn his praise into good council. He never flattered. Perhaps, too, it was just as well, for Christopher received that noon all the adulation that was good for him.

Corrigan, the big inspector, clapped him on the shoulders, calling him a little general; and Davis almost wrung his hand off. Even the silent Mr. Norcross announced he was a son to be proud of. As for Mr. Burton, Senior—well, he merely settled back into his office chair and beamed about him.

"I made no mistake when I christened that boy Christopher Mark Antony Burton, fourth," announced he, as if every whit of responsibility for the boy's good judgment were traceable to his name. "He has the stuff in him—has had since babyhood."

But Mr. Inspector did not wholly agree.

"You've got to do more than have good blood in your veins," he asserted, with a hint of scorn. "The young one used his brains, he did, and used 'em quick without thanks to his ancestors. Had he loitered about and depended on his great-grandfather, Stuart would have got away."

There was a general laugh, in which even Mr. Burton, chagrined though he was, joined.

Afterward the two police officers, Christopher, his father, Mr. Rhinehart, and Hollings rolled away to headquarters to identify the captured diamond thief.

CHAPTER IX
CHRISTOPHER RECOGNIZES
AN OLD ACQUAINTANCE

Yes, it was Stuart! There could be no possible doubt about that; nor, indeed, did the culprit attempt to deny his identity. Perhaps he realized that to do so would be futile. There he was in his wig, whiskers, glasses, ulster, and slouch hat; and the next moment, presto, valeted by Mr. Inspector, there he was in his fur coat—the elegant gentleman who had invaded Burton and Norcross' jewelry store!

Hollings recognized him in a twinkling and without a shade of hesitation singled him out from twelve other men; so, also, did Mr. Rhinehart and Christopher.

Poor Stuart! He was too genuine a sport to whine when he saw the game was up. On the contrary he assumed a good-natured, almost humorous stoicism, as if his capture were nothing more than a feature of the day's work. Only one fact regarding it did he appear to resent and that was that a person wary as himself should have been tracked down and trapped by a mere boy. Incontestably this wounded his pride. Nevertheless he tried valiantly to conceal his chagrin, maintaining throughout the ordeal of identification his jaunty pose and saluting Christopher, whom he instantly remembered having seen on the car, with a mocking bow and a smile of admiration.

"It was a neat trick you played me, youngster," announced he, as the lad approached. "They will be annexing you to the staff here if you don't look out."

"I had to do it, you know," Christopher answered, half apologizing for the double-faced rôle he had played. "I'm not usually a squealer—honest, I'm not. But the diamonds belonged to my father, and I saw you take them."

"Of course, sonny, of course. I'm not kicking—it was a fair game," the big fellow returned without a shadow of anger. "So you saw me take them, did you? Why didn't you sing out at the time?"

"It all happened so quickly that I could hardly trust my eyes," was the response. "Besides, you looked so much like a gentleman that I couldn't believe you were just a—a—"

"Thief," cut in Stuart sharply, supplying the word at which the boy had halted. Nevertheless despite the glibness with which he uttered it, he cringed and a flood of telltale color rose to his hair. It was the first time he had exhibited the slightest feeling.

Uncomfortably Christopher nodded.

"Well, that's what I am, you see," continued the man who had now regained his former debonnaire manner, "so the next time look out and don't be taken in. There are gentlemen who are thieves, sonny, and then again there are thieves who are gentlemen—at least I hope so."

So unruffled was his temper, so brave the front he put on the inevitable, that as Christopher saw him led away between two guards a momentary pang of regret passed over him. If Stuart had only happened to have turned his talents to some profession besides diamond stealing, what a delightful acquaintance he might have proved.

But the next instant Corrigan, the head inspector, broke in on this reverie, and his words banished further repining:

"The scoundrel won't open his lips," declared he to Mr. Burton. "What he's done with those diamonds we can't find out. He's mum as an oyster. I hoped we might tempt him into making a clean breast of the matter—but not he! He's too hardened a chap for repentance, I reckon."

"His pal, Tony, may have them."

"No doubt," acquiesced the chief. "The two probably have a cache where they stow their loot."

"I wish we could find it."

"So do I, with all my heart. We may, too, if we succeed in running down the other chap," Corrigan returned. "I shan't give up hope with Mr. Christopher on the job."

"I fancy my son isn't going into the business of tracking down criminals permanently," Burton, Senior, retorted a bit stiffly.

"Like enough not," came tartly from Corrigan.

"Still, he can keep his peepers open, eh, youngster?"

He smiled down upon Christopher from beneath his shaggy brows, and Christopher smiled back. There was something very likeable about Corrigan.

"I'll look alive," grinned the boy. "Only of course you know this kill was just a fluke."

The modest words evidently pleased the inspector.

"That's all right," said he. "You may make another. Who knows?"

He patted the lad's shoulder encouragingly and in friendly fashion added:

"Nobody bags a diamond robber every day."

They went out—Mr. Burton, his son, and the two clerks.

"We may as well go to luncheon now," announced Christopher's father, when the men had left them. "Where shall we go? We'll have a real celebration in honor of Stuart's capture."

"Poor Stuart!" murmured the lad.

"Mercy on us! Surely you are not regretting that you landed him in jail."

"No-o. Still, I'm sorry for him."

"Of course. We're always sorry to see a person of his ability go wrong. But he has only himself to thank for his fate. He might have known at the outset where he would bring up. They all are trapped sooner or later."

"I suppose so."

"Come, come, son! Don't go wasting any romantic sympathy on Stuart—or whatever his name is. He wouldn't appreciate it. Why, he would rob us again to-morrow if he got the chance," the head of the firm asserted harshly.

"Probably he would."

"You know he would."

"Y-es. But he was such a good sport."

"He knew there was nothing to be gained by whining and making himself disagreeable."

Nevertheless, in spite of his father's arguments, Christopher could not entirely put the unlucky Stuart out of his mind. Nor did the fried scallops, grilled sweet potatoes, and salad which his father ordered for him wholly blot out a lurking depression or the haunting memory of the criminal's face. It took two chocolate ice creams and an ample square of fudge cake to dispel his gloom and bring his spirits back to their accustomed cheerfulness.

By the time he and his father returned to the store, however, they were practically normal, and he ascended to the fourth floor to hunt up McPhearson, who amid the general excitement he had left somewhat abruptly.

"Well, so you landed your light-fingered friend, did you, laddie?" remarked the Scotchman.

"Mr. Corrigan did."

"It was thanks to you, I guess."

"Partly!"

"Humph! You don't seem very triumphant about it." The old man peered at the boy over the top of his glasses.

"I'm not. It made me sick—the whole thing."

"I know, sonny—I know. But we can't have such persons about," McPhearson said gently. "Of course you are sorry to put a fellow behind the bars, but—"

"He was so darned decent about it—and so plucky," exclaimed Christopher. "Why, he was almost a gentleman."

The sentence ended in a tremulous laugh.

"No doubt he may have started out to be a gentleman—poor chap—and then got on the wrong track. Well, you did what was right. You know that."

"I hope so," was the dull answer.

"We'll not talk about it any more. Come, let's shift the subject to something else."

"To clocks?"

"Aren't you tired of clocks?"

"No. Are you?"

"I never get tired of them," smiled McPhearson. "If I did, it would be fatal. They are my daily bread."

"And mine, too, for that matter," rejoined Christopher.

"Perhaps," admitted the Scotchman. "Still you do not subsist wholly on clocks. Your bread is studded with pearls, emeralds, and rubies."

The fancy pleased the boy, and he laughed.

"Rather indigestible eating," he protested.

"And yet you look fit as a king."

There was a moment's pause; then the man said:

"Well, if we are to talk clocks, where shall we begin?"

"Anywhere you like," returned the lad, with a shrug of his shoulders.

"Suppose, then, since you are so docile and accommodating, we leap to somewhere near the year 1650, when the inspiration to attach the pallets of the escapement to the pendulum rod, thereby making the escapement horizontal, came almost simultaneously to an Englishman named Harris and a Dutchman named Huyghens. These, together with the later ideas of anchor escapement evolved by Graham, put clocks, within the span of a few years, on an almost modern basis. Other improvements such as using steel springs in place of weights and the perfecting of movements have of course been made since; but this period covers the time of most vital improvement in the art of clockmaking. At this time, too, some of the finest of old English watches and clocks were made. Thomas Tompion, sometimes called the father of English clock making, took his place at the head of these, and to this day beautiful old clocks that are still in service testify to his skillful workmanship."

"What sort of clocks did he make?" inquired Christopher with interest.

"Just about every design of the period—bracket clocks similar to those of Richard Parsons'; long-case, or what we call grandfather, clocks; even brass clocks with projecting dials; and in addition, the greater part of the finest watches turned out at this time were of his making. There were few who could equal him. Possibly Daniel Quare and Joseph Knibb made clocks as good, but they certainly made no better. Were you to visit Buckingham Palace or Windsor Castle, you would find there wonderful chiming grandfather clocks made by this same Thomas Tompion. They are genuine treasures and would bring almost any price. So remember, in journeying through the world, if you ever run across a clock or a watch made by Thomas Tompion, you are looking at a very fine bit of handicraft."

"I'm afraid I never shall," Christopher shook his head.

"One never can tell where his path through life will take him," McPhearson said. "For example, I never expected my wanderings would lead me from Glasgow to America. Nor, probably, did Stuart dream when he woke up to-day that his morning ride in a Fifth Avenue bus would land him in jail. So you must not despair of seeing London and some of Thomas Tompion's clocks. Moreover, should you go there, I hope you will hunt up in Westminster Abbey the grave of this famous man."

"Was he buried at Westminster? Why, I thought only kings, queens, poets, and great people had places there," Christopher ventured, a trifle incredulous.

"Usually they do, but Thomas Tompion well merited the honor due him, I assure you. To begin with, he was no ordinary tradesman. He was a person of culture who all his life associated with the foremost philosophers and mathematicians of his day. So widely was his ability recognized that he was made leading watchmaker to the court of Charles II. Now, although timekeepers had vastly improved, they were still pretty faulty, experimental contrivances, whose outside trappings counted with the public far more than did their interior mechanism. Tompion changed all this. Seizing upon all that was good offered by the inventors preceding him, he carefully re-proportioned the various parts and produced English clocks and watches that were at once the pride and despair of his brother craftsmen. Watches were something of an avocation with him, for his primary trade was in clocks, to which for many years he devoted his entire labor. Probably, however, the problems a watch presented won his interest and led him to try his skill in this new field, with the result that he was soon making watches that as far surpassed his associates' as did his clocks. He made a watch for the king, the fame of which traveled to France and prompted the Dauphin to order two like it. These watches all had two balances and balance springs fashioned after the scheme Hooke had worked out. They also, like most of Tompion's timekeepers, had an hour and a minute hand. One more innovation which he presented (and it was a very practical one) was the numbering of his watch movements for purposes of identification—a plan very generally followed since by present-day workmen. And yet all this which I have told you does not give you half an idea of what Tompion really was."

McPhearson paused thoughtfully.

"Thomas Tompion stood for something more than any of these things. He was a genuine lover of his art, and when we see or read of the many kinds of clocks and watches he produced, we cannot but feel the joy he had in making them. He made, for example, a marvellous clock that would run a year without winding, which William III had in his bedroom at Kensington Palace, it having been left to him by the Earl of Leicester. This clock, although small, struck the hours and quarter-hours, and was of ebony with silver mountings. And to prove to you that it was no novelty timepiece to be used merely for ornament, I will tell you that now, after a hundred and fifty years, it is still running and faithfully doing its duty."

"Who owns it?" queried Christopher.

"It has for a century and a half been in the possession of the family of Lord Mostyn and so famous has been its history that this nobleman has kept the names of those who have wound it during the last hundred years."

"All sorts of bigwigs, I suppose," put in Christopher.

"A list of celebrated persons, you may be sure."

"Was Ebenezer on it?" Christopher chuckled mischievously.

"Most likely he would have been had he not been so busy winding Mr. Hawley's treasures," replied the Scotchman, smiling at the jest. "Then in 1695 Tompion made a very fine traveling striking and alarm watch with case beautifully chased. The Pump Room at Bath boasts a tall clock of his make—a present from him to the city in acknowledgment of the benefits he derived from its mineral waters. There are also examples of his craft in famous clock collections both here and in England, the Wetherfield collection owning eighteen made by him."

"And did his tall clocks have weights?"

"Yes, their driving power was a big lead weight. The clock at Bath has a thirty-two-pound weight of lead which drops monthly six feet."

"Is it only wound each month?"

"That's all. Some of these tall clocks made by Tompion ran a year without winding. Nor must you get the impression that clocks and watches were the only things this remarkable mechanic produced, for at Hampton Court is a barometer of his construction, proving him to be a master of more intricate science than the mere art of time-keeping. In fact many of his clocks show the days and the months, as well as the difference between sun time and mean time."

"I don't quite understand what mean time is. Isn't all time alike?"

"Mercy, no! Sun time and our time are two quite different things. Some day I will tell you why. Of this Thomas Tompion, although he lived long ago, was well aware. You see, therefore, he was no ordinary uneducated clockmaker. What wonder that he and George Graham, one of the illustrious pupils he trained, should have been buried together at Westminster Abbey!"

"You haven't told me anything about Graham."

"He was a nephew of Tompion and a very clever craftsman whose clocks did honor to his teacher. *Honest George Graham,* he was called—not a bad way to come down through history. Personally I would rather have that handle before my name than to have *Lord* or *Duke* precede it and I fancy George Graham was of a type who felt that way too! So devoted were he and Tompion and so closely linked was their work that when Graham died, the grave of Tompion was opened in order that the two men might be buried together. Then a stone was made reading:

> Here lies the body of Mr. Tho. Tompion who departed this life the 20th of November 1713 in the 75th year of his age.
>
> ———————————————
>
> Also the body of George Graham of London watchmaker and F.R.S. whose curious inventions do honour to ye British genius whose accurate performances are ye standard of Mechanic Skill. He died ye XVI of November MDCCLI in the LXXVIII year of his age.

"Now a bit of interesting history is attached to this stone. Several years after it had been put in place a younger generation came along who knew very little of either Tompion or his pupil Graham, and seeing the large tablet, some of them decided to take it up and put instead smaller stones with only the inscriptions:

MR. T. TOMPION 1713
MR. G. GRAHAM 1751

upon them. Perhaps the authorities felt the big stone took up too much room; or perhaps they felt it heaped undue honor on two men who in their estimation were really nothing but tradesmen; or, worse yet, perhaps they had forgotten all Tompion and Graham did for the rest of us. However that may be, in 1842 a Bond Street watchmaker had loyalty and courage enough to protest, and through the late Dean Stanley the old stone, fortunately uninjured, was hunted up and reinstated in its original position, thereby proving that England does not after all forget her debt to these splendidly intelligent workmen."

"I'm glad the first stone was put back," Christopher asserted. "Who on earth would ever know from the skimpy marking on the other one who Mr. T. Tompion or Mr. G. Graham were?"

"Probably very few persons—only those, most likely, who had made a study of clocks. To my mind it is far better to remind the ignorant who perhaps never heard of Tompion or Graham, to hold their memory in grateful respect. Possibly, too, the inscription on the tablet may prompt the casual passer-by to look up what these two men did, and if so a keener appreciation of them will be established."

"I shall go and see that stone if I ever go to London," Christopher declared.

"Do, laddie. And see some of their clocks, too. Graham was a clever, broadly educated man, who worked out many astronomical instruments in addition to his clockmaking. When you view either his handiwork or that of Tompion, you will see the product of master craftsmen. And in the meantime don't forget Daniel Quare, Samuel Knibb, or Ahasuerus Fromanteel, who although unhonored by stones in the Abbey, are well worthy of being remembered."

CHAPTER X
AN AMAZING ADVENTURE

WITHIN a day or two Christopher was once more reminded of the diamond robbery by having Corrigan call up the firm and announce that Stuart, wanted in Chicago for the rifling of a safe, had been taken west under guard.

"As yet," concluded the inspector, "we have made no progress toward the recovery of the ring. It has neither put in its appearance at any of the pawnshops nor have we been able to trace the stones. We do not, however, despair of getting some clew and shall still keep on the lookout."

"I suppose you have no track of Tony—Stuart's accomplice, either?" inquired Mr. Burton over the wire.

"None, I am sorry to say."

With a sigh of discouragement the senior partner hung up the receiver.

"I guess the incident is as good as closed," remarked he. "In my opinion we can bid good-by to those diamonds and accept our burglar insurance with thankfulness that our loss was not greater."

"But Stuart's pal may show up yet, Dad," ventured the optimistic Christopher, who chanced at the moment to be in the office.

"I doubt it." Skeptically Mr. Burton shook his head. "More

likely he has decided New York is too hot for him and has left town for pastures new."

"He may be lying low," asserted the habitually silent Mr. Norcross.

"Possibly."

Nevertheless, despite his acquiescence, Mr. Burton returned to his letters with an air indicative that at least, so far as he was concerned, the possibility he granted was an exceedingly remote one—too remote to merit further consideration.

And indeed it did appear to be so until one day, like a meteor out of the heavens, a grimy communication postmarked Chicago was brought to Christopher, who in a fit of boredom was roaming aimlessly about the lamp department.

"I guess this is meant for you, Mr. Christopher," announced the messenger, whose duty it was to distribute the store mail. "Funny way to address it, though. You'd take it for a valentine:

Mr. Burton's son
Care Burton and Norcross, Jewellers,
New York City."

"That's me all right," cried Christopher, forgetting in his excitement and curiosity such a trivial incidental as grammar.

He took the letter, regarding with amusement its disreputable appearance.

"Humph! They didn't waste very dressy stationery on me, did they?" laughed he.

"It isn't deckle-edge paper with a ducal seal, if that is what you're expecting," grinned the boy, not unwilling to air his knowledge of such matters.

As with an impish grimace he disappeared Christopher tore

open the envelope he held and drew from it a single crushed manilla sheet on which was scrawled:

> I told you it was not impossible for a thief to be a gentleman, and to prove it, I am tipping you off about that ring. I wouldn't do this either for your father or for Corrigan, but you're such a decent little chap I'd like you to have the thing back again. Besides, as I am in quod for a long term, the sparklers will do me no good. At 184 Speedwell St. (Suite 6) I hold a room under the name of Carlton. You will find the loot hidden in the floor-ing under a narrow board between the radiator and the window. The police will be only too glad to help you reclaim it. There are a few other trinkets there too they will like to have. The stuff is all mine. I quarreled with my pal after the affair at your father's store, and since then have been playing a lone game. Good luck to you, little chap. Maybe if I'd started out with your chance, I should not be where I am to-day. I wish to Heaven I had.

Twice Christopher read the letter, his eyes wide, and his throat a bit choky with emotion. To say he was surprised at the contents of the strange communication would have been to put it mildly. Not only was he astounded, he was somewhat incredulous. And yet, overmastering this disbelief was a certainty that the writer of the letter was speaking the truth. Urged on by some whim of his own, some impulse so subtle it defied analysis, Stuart was returning the property he had stolen. Perhaps remorse had overtaken him; perhaps shame; or possibly these gentler motives did but mingle with the realization that the gems, as he himself asserted, would now be useless to him. At any rate, repentant or not, here he was giving them back to their rightful owner!

What wonder the letter needed neither salutation nor signature to identify its sender? That Stuart had penned the note and contrived to find some one he could trust to mail it was obvious. And yet Christopher, fingering it, could not but speculate as to how it had struggled to freedom. Through what strange hands had it passed,—what mazes of strategy and concealment? Ah, it was futile to attempt to trace its devious trail. Here it was in his possession, and with a sudden inrush of joy, his bewildered senses stirred to action, and he hastened with his tidings to his father's office, where he burst in on Mr. Burton in the act of dictating a letter:

"Oh, Dad!" ejaculated he. "I've the biggest sort of a surprise for you. He's written me! Think of that! Written to say where it is."

"Christopher!" thundered his father. "What do you mean by dashing in here like a madman and interrupting my work? Have you forgotten this is my private office? Offer your apologies to me and to Miss Elkins and then sit down and wait until I am at leisure."

"I'm sorry, Dad. I was so excited that—"

"There, there! That will do. You don't need to tell me you are excited. Pray calm yourself and sit down quietly until I am at liberty to hear what you have to say."

"Yes, sir."

Crestfallen, the boy sank into a big leather chair in a dim corner of the room.

"and in reply advise you that shipment billed to us via S.S. *George Washington* has been received, and is in every way satisfactory. We will remit payment as usual through our Amsterdam brokers.

"Appreciating your courteous and reliable service, I remain,
Truly yours,
Christopher Mark Antony Burton, third."

Mr. Burton came to a stop and leaned back in his massive mahogany chair.

"There, Miss Elkins, get that off immediately," ordered he. "Also the two cablegrams I dictated. That will be all at present. Now, Christopher, suppose you give me your mighty tidings."

A faint note of sarcasm, not lost on the boy, echoed in the words, and with enthusiasm quenched, the lad silently produced his note and laid it on his father's desk.

"What's this?" Mr. Burton asked.

"You can read it."

"A vilely dirty scrap of paper. What have you been doing with it—cleaning your shoes?"

"It was that way when it came."

"Came? Came from whom?"

"Read it and see."

"But the thing has neither beginning nor end. Was it meant for you?"

"Yes, sir. It came through the mail."

Taking the envelope from his pocket, Christopher placed it beside the letter.

Mr. Burton, however, did not heed either object.

Instead, with deliberation, he took off his glasses, wiped them and put them back on his nose. Then he lighted a fresh cigar. Even an observer less keen than his son could have detected that the major portion of his mind was still occupied by the cablegrams and dictation that had previously engaged him, and that he anticipated no very vital disclosures from the morsel of grimy paper he so gingerly took up.

Slowly he read it. Then the boy, watching, saw his figure become tense, and a flash of amazement light his eyes.

"Great Heavens!" cried he, startled out of his customary dignity. "It's from Stuart. Why didn't you say so at once?"

"I tried to tell you."

"Yes, yes. I know! But I had no idea you had anything as important as this to say. If you had only explained—"

"I was going to, only you—"

"Well, we won't stop to discuss all that now. I'll call Corrigan immediately. I don't suppose there is any chance but the note is genuine. Why, it would be a seven-days' wonder if we should get those stones back. The insurance money was no compensation for them. We could not buy three such perfectly matched diamonds had we ten times their price. Of course there is a possibility this letter may be a fake, but somehow I've a feeling it is real. We'll consult Corrigan and see what he says."

Mr. Burton reached for the telephone.

"Hello! Give me Plaza 77098.—Is Mr. Corrigan there?—Just going out?—Catch him before he leaves, and tell him, please, that Mr. Burton wishes to speak with him." A pause followed, in which Mr. Burton nervously drummed on his desk. Then he leaned forward expectantly. "Mr. Corrigan? This is Mr. Burton speaking. I've some news for you. My son has this morning received from Chicago a letter purporting to come from Stuart and giving the location of that ring.—Of course it may be— What's that?—You are on your way up to this vicinity? That will be very nice then.—Yes, eleven will suit us all right. Good-by."

"He is coming up, is he?"

"Yes. He happened to be coming, anyway. A queer thing—that letter. I hardly know what to think about it."

"Nor I."

"I certainly never heard of a thief relenting and returning his spoils."

"I'm afraid he doesn't—usually," smiled Christopher.

"Then why do it this time?" mused Burton, Senior, pondering the mystery.

"You've got me, unless, as Stuart himself explains, he is in for a long prison term and knows the diamonds won't do him any good."

"But he could leave them where they are and run the chance of finding them when he gets out. If they are well concealed it is unlikely anybody would discover them. I don't get it at all."

Scowling, Mr. Burton lapsed into a silence so forbidding that Christopher dared not interrupt it, and accordingly the two sat without speaking until Mr. Corrigan was announced.

It took not a moment to see the inspector was more than wontedly excited.

"Where is this remarkable communication?" demanded he without preliminary. "Humph! Looks as though it had been through the wars, doesn't it! A scrap of paper some convict had concealed, most likely, together with the stump of a pencil. Those fellows are pretty clever; and Stuart probably got some chap whose sentence was up to mail it when he went out. He would hardly risk sending information like this by anybody except one of his own kind. And even then he would have to be pretty certain his messenger could be trusted. It was taking a big chance. Sometimes, however, there is honor among thieves."

"Do you think the letter is genuine?" inquired Mr. Burton.

"How, genuine? That it tells the truth, you mean? Yes, I do. I think Stuart was prompted to return the ring for the very reasons he states—he took a fancy to Christopher, and he saw the diamonds would now be of no use to him."

"But he could have left them where they are."

"For a term of ten or twelve years? But think, Mr. Burton, of the changes liable to take place in that time. The building might be torn down and replaced by another, or it might be converted into a business block; or, again, fire might destroy it. In any of these cases the jewels would be lost to Stuart. Moreover, even if he tried to recover them years hence, it might be very difficult to do so. He weighed all these considerations, you may be sure, before he sent that letter. Still I am not sure they were the factors primarily influencing him. He liked Christopher and evidently wished to do him a good turn. Such men as he often have soft streaks in them—impulses for good."

"You mean to follow up the clew then?"

"Mean to follow it up? Man alive! Certainly I do. And what is more, I mean to lose no time in doing it," answered Corrigan, rising.

"I wish—" began Christopher, and then stopped.

"You wish you could go along?" asked the inspector, turning toward the lad with a friendly smile.

"That is what I was going to say—yes."

"Well, we'll take you. I think you've earned the right to be in at the finish."

"Really!" cried Christopher.

"Sure thing."

"Do you think he'd better go?" Mr. Burton queried, instantly anxious. "You hardly know what you are going to get into. It may be a trap of some sort. Suppose, as a matter of revenge, there were a bomb under the floor."

"I'm not doing any worrying on that score," responded the inspector. "Had Stuart sent the note to you or to me, I should be on my guard; but as it has come to Christopher, I have no fears. Of course, however, I shall take every precaution."

"I hope so, for the sake of every one concerned."

"Oh, I shall be careful, Mr. Burton. Don't you worry about that. I have my eye teeth cut."

"When do you mean to take up the affair?"

"This minute! As soon as I can get my men together and the necessary formalities disposed of."

"Am I to go right along with you?" Christopher leaped to his feet.

"Yes. Fetch your hat and coat. I'll take care of the boy, Mr. Burton. Have no concern about him. It is only natural he should wish to see this job through, having been mixed up in it from the first. Besides, remember we have him to thank for every clew we have succeeded in getting. It was he who witnessed the robbery; he who trapped and identified Stuart; he who now furnishes us with the whereabouts of the loot. You wouldn't deprive him of seeing the end of the drama, would you?"

"No-o," answered Mr. Burton slowly. "Still, it is no place for him. He's been mixed up with criminals and police stations ever since he came into this store. I didn't bring him here for any such purpose. Why, he has secured more knowledge of thieves and prisons during the last few weeks than he would have gathered together in a lifetime."

"He may be the wiser for it, too. Have you thought of that? Crime isn't very attractive when one sees this side of it."

"That is true," agreed Burton, Senior.

"Let Christopher alone, Mr. Burton. What he has seen won't hurt him. It has been a grim, sad adventure in which it would be hard to find one alluring feature."

"I guess that is true. Certainly evil has not triumphed."

"It never does—in the long run," declared Corrigan emphatically. "I've seen the thing over and over again, and have followed the history of most of the men we have tracked down. Sooner or later they are brought to justice. In the meantime they lead the lives of hunted foxes, never knowing a safe or peaceful moment. Some may call that happiness, but I don't. When you make of yourself an outlaw and cut yourself off from the big universe of decent people, you sentence yourself to a pretty wretched, lonely life. Even the worst of criminals often wish themselves back into that world they have left behind them, and which they know for a certainty they never can enter again."

"Stuart seemed to in his letter."

"That's exactly what I mean. Even Stuart, who has been at this sort of thing since he was a young lad, isn't contented with the lot he has chosen. Could he start over, he would follow the other path. He as good as says so himself. They are all like that when you get them at their best moments. That is why I am so sure this note to Christopher tells the truth. It is the voice of Stuart sighing for what might have been."

"Have you any idea where this street he mentions is?" interrogated Mr. Burton.

"Oh, yes. It is up in Harlem. A very decent locality. We shall have no trouble. Doubtless the people of whom he hired his room thought him a gentleman. He could ape one when he tried. Moreover, he had a good deal of the gentleman in him. Probably were we able to dig out his ancestry, we should find he came of excellent parentage. He's a gentleman gone wrong."

"It's a pity."

"It's worse than that, Mr. Burton. It is a tragedy," declared Corrigan, as he and Christopher went out.

CHAPTER XI
THE SEQUEL TO THE LETTER

ONE hundred eighty-four Speedwell Street proved to be a trim, well-kept apartment leased by a clerk in one of the large dry-goods houses and occupied by himself, his wife, his sister and two children. The family was of French descent and was thrifty and respectable. In order to make both ends of their slender income meet they had taken as a boarder Mr. Carlton (alias Stuart) whom they had found to be a delightful addition to the household.

"Yes, indeed! We know Monsieur Carlton well," replied the pretty little wife in response to Corrigan's inquiries. "He is charming. Such a gentleman and so kind to the children! But he is away just now. In fact, we have heard nothing from him for several days and were becoming a trifle worried by his silence. I hope no ill has befallen him." Apprehensively her eye traveled with questioning gaze over the inspector's blue uniform.

"I am afraid your boarder will not be back for some time," responded he not unkindly.

"Something has happened to him then. *Mon Dieu!* I am sorry—sorry! The children will break their hearts crying. Has he been hurt? Or maybe he is ill?"

"No, it is nothing of that sort. Later I will explain it all to you. He sent us to get something he had left here."

"To be sure. Come in, won't you? Ah, I am glad he is not sick! See, this is his room. We gave him our best one because he liked it and could pay."

"May I bring in some men who accompanied me?" asked Corrigan gently.

"Surely! Whatever you wish you may do since you are Mr. Carlton's friend. But I do not at all understand what is the trouble. Can't you—"

"By and by, madam, you shall know."

"It must, of course, be as you wish," agreed the tiny French woman with a smile. "I know nothing about it. Why should I interfere? Will you and your companions please step this way?" Then with surprise, "What, more police?"

"Yes. But you must not be afraid," the inspector declared reassuringly. "We want nothing of you. Only what Mr.—"

"Carlton—"

"Mr. Carlton sent us to secure," concluded Corrigan.

"Eh, *bien*! Enter then. This is the way. It is here Mr. Carlton sleeps. A pleasant room, you see. Books, magazines, and even a plant in bloom. He is fond of flowers."

"I am not surprised," murmured Corrigan with a shrug. "A gentleman—as I asserted. The radiator is here. Tim. That must be the board. Take it up carefully so not to splinter it and deface the flooring. No doubt it will come easily."

"The floor—you are not going to tear up the floor!" cried the woman excitedly.

"Only one board," was the soothing answer. "We shall do no injury to your premises."

"But surely Mr. Carlton would not hide things away under the floor; only thieves do that." She laughed a tremulous, half-frightened laugh at the absurdity of the jest.

"How about it, Tim? Is it coming?" questioned Corrigan, ignoring the pleasantry.

"It stirs, sir; but it is not so loose as you might expect. Didn't Blake bring a chisel?"

"Yes, it's here. Why not run a knife down that crack and see if you can't raise the board a little. If you can lift it enough to slip something under it will come up," directed the chief.

"It's coming now, sir. There, we have it!"

"Take out all those wads of tissue paper."

"Here they are, sir."

"Any more?"

"I reckon not, sir."

"Still, you'd better make sure. Run your hand in at each end as far as you can reach."

"There's nothing there, sir. A beam goes along where those nails are."

"You are sure there is no other opening?"

"Certain of it."

"Nevertheless, I'll have a look myself."

"To be sure, Mr. Corrigan," the officer replied, stepping aside.

Carefully the chief stooped down and explored the chasm with his hand.

"You're right, Tim; there is nothing more," asserted he. "We have everything we came after, I guess."

"I am glad to hear that," put in the French woman with returning confidence. "Mr. Carlton will, I am sure, be pleased that you found what he sent you for. But what a strange place for him to store his property! Things of value, no doubt, which he treasured and feared might be lost. Have you any idea when he will be back? Perhaps if you would give me his address I might write him a letter—that is, if you think—" She halted timidly.

For the fraction of a second Corrigan was silent as if he winced at performing the duty before him.

"I am afraid, madam," responded he at last, "that Mr. Carlton will not return; nor, I fear, will you wish him back when you know the circumstances under which he has disappeared. Suffice it to say we come vested with authority to take possession of his personal effects. After to-day there will be no need for you to reserve his room."

"You mean he is not to return at all—*never?*" asked the woman in an awe-stricken voice.

Corrigan nodded.

Weakly the woman dropped into a chair, a sudden light of pained understanding breaking over her face.

"You mean Mr. Carlton—"

"That was not his real name," interrupted the officer. "He went under several names. Stuart is the one the police know him by. He was a professional diamond thief."

"No, no! I cannot believe it," protested the loyal little creature stoutly. "Why, he was all kindness to us. When my husband was ill he nursed him for a whole week, day and night. He gave toys to the children, did errands, and often brought us fruit or candy. Are you sure there is no mistake? Certainly we should know if he were a bad man."

"Alas, my good woman, the proofs we hold in our hands are so convincing as to leave not the slightest possibility for error. There were, you see, two Carltons—the kind, friendly gentleman you knew; and the clever, experienced criminal with whom the police were acquainted. Most of us are a combination of various selves. This man had two sharply contrasting individualities and unfortunately it was the baser of them that dominated. He has a long prison record behind him."

"*Ciel!*" The woman clasped her hands in horror. "But why?" exclaimed she. "He did not need to steal. He always had plenty of money."

"That was how he got it."

For a while she seemed too stunned to say more; then she whispered:

"And where is he now?"

"Serving a prison sentence for a crime in Chicago."

"It is terrible—terrible! Oh, my husband will be sad to hear this; and my sister too. Poor fellow! I can scarcely believe it. Suppose the neighbors were to hear we had been housing a burglar—they would not speak to us."

"No one will know unless you yourself tell them," the inspector answered.

"Ah, you may be sure I shall not do that," was the instant response. "Not even my children will I tell. They were fond of Mr. Carlton."

"Let them remain so. It can do no harm. In fact, no doubt the man they loved merited their affection," answered the inspector. "I wish he had been just that and nothing else."

"And so do I—with all my heart!"

In the meantime, while Corrigan had been occupied with Stuart's landlady two bluecoats had been ransacking the closet and searching the contents of a trunk that stood in the room. Here they had brought to light a bag of tools and a variety of garments, hats, and wigs evidently used as disguises.

As they now displayed these trophies before the eyes of the bewildered French woman, the last vestige of hope she had cherished vanished and she burst into tears.

"Alas, alas!" sobbed she. "He was a bad man. I am convinced of it now. And yet I cannot believe he was entirely bad."

"No one is all bad—thank Heaven," the chief responded, as he gathered together the things that had been found, sent his men below, and having said farewell, closed the door upon the weeping French woman. Then, as he and Christopher went soberly downstairs, he added:

"Poor woman—she was all cut up. Everybody who goes wrong breaks somebody's heart. He's bound to. The destinies of all of us are so entangled with other persons that there is no such thing as living only to ourselves. Consider, for example, how many individuals this Stuart came in contact with—your father, yourself, Hollings, Rhinehart, and these unlucky French people. He might as well have touched those lives for good as for evil. And we are only a small part of the men and women he has run up against during his existence. When I think of that, it turns me pretty sober. The influence each of us exerts reaches a so much wider circle than we realize that it certainly behooves us to make the power we hold as strong for good as we are able, doesn't it?"

Christopher nodded gravely. Little more was said until the Burton and Norcross store was reached, where, parting from their blue-uniformed companions, Christopher and the inspector ascended to the firm's private offices. Here on the desk of the senior partner Corrigan proceeded to unwrap and display the treasure he had recovered. There was a sparkling diamond pendant, two or three broaches, a sapphire-studded bracelet, and the much-lamented and long-sought-for ring.

"You can identify it, can you, Mr. Burton?" questioned the officer, as he passed it over for examination.

"Anywhere on earth, I believe," replied the jeweler. "The setting has not even been disturbed. Nevertheless, to make certainty more sure, let us send for Hollings and for Rhinehart, our expert."

"By all means."

Mr. Burton touched a bell and gave the order and while waiting for it to be obeyed sat regarding the heap of flashing baubles lying before him.

"Somebody beside ourselves will rejoice to see their property coming back," mused he. "I wonder who these other things belong to. That pendant is a very fine one."

"Without looking up the description I am fairly certain the pendant is one lost by a guest at the Biltmore. We have been on the hunt for it some time. The other jewels may also belong to the same party. Quite a list of missing articles was given us. I have it down at headquarters."

"Well, if the owners are as much gratified to see their diamonds returning as we are—"

The opening of the door cut short further comment and Hollings and Mr. Rhinehart came into the room. It was evident from their manner they had no inkling as to why they had been summoned and the former employee, fearful of another disaster, was pallid with apprehension.

"Ever see this ring before, Hollings?" questioned Mr. Burton, whirling round in his swivel chair and extending the jewel.

"My soul, sir! You don't mean—" He stopped, speechless.

"What do you say, Mr. Rhinehart?"

"It certainly looks like our property," declared the more cautious clerk. "If it is, the identification letters BNC will be found scratched inside the band of the ring. Have you a glass there?"

"Mr. Rhinehart isn't going to commit himself without a microscope," chuckled the inspector. "He is dead right too."

"I wish to verify the stones as well as the setting," replied the expert.

"I guess in this case your stones are genuine enough. Stuart hadn't much chance to tamper with them. Nevertheless, it can do no harm to make sure," Corrigan said.

Opening a drawer Mr. Burton produced a powerful glass which he handed to Rhinehart who went to the light and carefully scanned the scintillating gems.

"Flawless and of the first water!" exclaimed he, after a tense pause. "The setting hasn't been touched, so there is practically no danger of substitution."

"You mean we have actually got the ring back—diamonds and all?" put in Hollings, as if unable to make real the miracle.

"We have—thanks to Mr. Corrigan," was Mr. Burton's reply.

"Thanks to young Christopher, you mean, sir," smiled the chief protestingly.

"What can I do to thank you?" cried Hollings. "I said I would give anything I possessed if those diamonds could be reclaimed and I'm ready to live up to my promise."

"Pooh, pooh!" laughed Corrigan. "I've no wish for payment, man. To win out in this game is payment enough for me. Besides, the police are not allowed to accept money, you know. An officer of the law gets his satisfaction in clearing up a crime and locating the loot. Until he can do that his mind is never at peace. This day's stroke has enabled me to wipe two mysteries that have balked me off my slate and go to bed to-night with at least that many less on my mind."

He rose.

"Well, Chief, all I can say is that we are very grateful to you," declared Mr. Burton.

He would have said more had not the inspector raised his hand with a forbidding gesture.

"It's all right, sir. I'm fully as glad as you to see your property safely returned. If you have any thanks to bestow, pass them on to your son, for without him the missing diamonds might never have been located."

Then turning toward the boy he added:

"Should you want a job on the force, youngster, come down to headquarters. A lad who can win the hearts of criminals and coax them into voluntarily returning their ill-gotten gains would be an immense asset in our business."

Shaking hands all round and clapping Christopher affectionately on the shoulder, the chief went out.

"Better put that ring back in the show case, Hollings," concluded Mr. Burton. "I don't need to caution you to keep an eye on it, I guess."

"You bet you don't!" was the fervent ejaculation. Then Hollings blushed to the roots of his hair at having thus addressed the great Mr. Burton.

But for once that worthy appeared to forget his dignity and, becoming human, he laughed like a boy of ten.

CHAPTER XII

CLOCK GIANTS

RADUALLY the excitement concerning the diamond robbery died away as do ripples in a pool and once more Christopher found himself settling down on the little wooden stool at McPhearson's elbow. The two had by this time become great friends, the boy preferring the companionship of the little Scotchman to that of any one else in the store. Perhaps this preference grew in a measure out of the fact that McPhearson appeared to like him and make more effort to entertain him than did the other clerks; perhaps also he had discovered that the clockmaker, when he did speak, was better worth listening to.

Be that as it may, he sallied into the repair department very glad to be there again.

"I feel as if I hadn't had a clock lesson for ages," observed he, as he sat down.

"Clock lesson? What do you mean?" The man with the swift-moving hands shot him a quick, puzzled glance.

"Oh, don't think I am here to steal your trade," retorted Christopher mischievously. "I only mean that so far as I am concerned the clock world stopped with Quare, Tompion, and Graham."

"Indeed it didn't," contradicted the Scotchman, instantly

bristling. "Though if it had, you would not need to be pitied for those makers would have bequeathed you some pretty fine products. And when you consider that Tompion, at least, began life as a blacksmith it is the more remarkable. Think what it meant to work out of such a crude, rough trade into one so delicate! Still, it was an age of marvels—a strange, fantastic, interesting era in which to have lived. Many members of the Clockmakers' Company were blacksmiths who had graduated into this higher calling and now boasted their own shops and apprentices. These latter men helped about under supervision, learning the trade and completing from eight to ten years of service before being taken in turn into the guild and permitted to make clocks. In the meantime they prepared simple parts of the work and made themselves useful in any direction they were able, even running errands or standing at the shop door and coaxing the passers-by to come in and purchase."

"Pretty primitive advertising," smiled Christopher.

"Advertising was primitive in those days," agreed McPhearson. "Sometimes when trade was dull the unfortunate apprentices were sent out to tour the streets and bring in customers. Or the present of a watch or clock would be made to the king or some nobleman of wealth and influence in the hope that such a gift would stimulate others to buy. No doubt even the celebrated Graham, in the days of his apprenticeship to Tompion, may have had some of these humble duties to perform. But if so they failed to dash his enthusiasm for his profession, for you see how well he profited by his teaching and what a master at clockmaking he finally became. He had always been an ingenious fellow interested in evolving mathematical instruments of all sorts."

"Were his clocks as good as Tompion's?" queried Christopher.

"As to that, the two were pretty well matched," was the

answer. "Graham, however, concentrated most of his skill on watches while Tompion put the major part of his talent into long-case clocks which were unrivaled. For, by this time, with the gradual development and improvement of clock machinery, it was possible to make grandfather, or long-case, clocks that kept excellent time. The defects of the old wheel escapement of the thirteenth, fourteenth, and fifteenth centuries were, as I told you, remedied in part by the invention of the fusee, a device for equalizing the movement. Then came the conversion of such clocks into pendulum clocks—no very difficult matter. One of the balls on the verge was removed, thereby making the verge longer and increasing the weight of the other ball. Then such clocks, together with those having a crown wheel escapement, went in turn out of vogue and the anchor escapement ushered in what is commonly known as the grandfather clock. It was in producing this particular type of timepiece that Tompion and Graham excelled. The pendulum was hung from a thin steel spring instead of being placed on an axis carrying pallets and could swing without friction."

"And whose scheme was that?"

"It is generally conceded that a Dutchman by the name of Fromanteel brought the modern pendulum idea into England. You will recall that early in clock history there were some pendulums of a very unsatisfactory nature in use—pendulums that were regulated by weights and dangled at the back or across the front of old brass clocks."

"I remember, yes."

"Well, it was that same pendulum principle carried to greater perfection and now scientifically applied which made the present grandfather, or long-case, clock possible. Certainly Fromanteel did a vast service to English clockmaking when he brought this solution of the pendulum problem to London, for with the anchor, or dead-beat escapement, combined with a long pendulum terminating in a heavy bob, the force of gravity caused such slight variation that the motion was practically harmonic and had only a very minor effect on the clock. For a long case, you see, has an exceedingly confined arc of oscillation because the swing of the pendulum is so limited. It is this length of pendulum together with its almost harmonic motion which results in the excellent time-keeping done by clocks of the "grandfather" class. The time a pendulum takes to vibrate always depends on its length—that is, the distance between the center of suspension and the center of gravity of the bob."

McPhearson paused to hold to the light a small brass pivot he was filing.

"Just here," continued he, "we stumble upon still another of the multiple tribulations of the clockmaker. If a big clock is expected to do any very fine work the latitude of the place in which it is to be put must be taken into consideration. For example, experiment has proved that the length of a pendulum vibrating seconds at London will not serve as accurately in other latitudes, because according to the laws of gravity the length of seconds increases in a specific ratio as we advance from the equator toward the poles. The clockmaker must, therefore, take care to regulate the length of his pendulum to correspond with this law."

"Great Scott! Why, I never dreamed there was so much to clockmaking!" gasped the astonished Christopher.

"Oh, the making of a finely adjusted, close-running clock is far more of a science than a trade, laddie. It isn't just making a lot of wheels that will turn, hands that will point, or a mechanism that will tick—wonderful as all that is," asserted McPhearson.

"I don't believe most persons realize it isn't."

"Those who dip below the surface and are better informed know the truth; as for the others—we must not expect too much of a hurrying world, son. Any branch of knowledge takes us very far if we follow it to the end. Why, look at me! I have spent all my life with clocks and what do I know about them?"

"A great deal," was the prompt retort.

"Very little, my boy; very little indeed!" sighed the old man. "I couldn't make one. Nevertheless I have had great pleasure in hunting down what I have learned. It is an interesting subject and one that never seems to exhaust itself. For all the wonders of my trade are not yet told. When, for instance, they put the clock on the Metropolitan Life Insurance building here in New York an undreamed-of pinnacle in clock construction was reached. There was a time when the clock on the London Houses of Parliament was the last word in the art—a veritable triumph of the horologe. Not only was it the largest timepiece in the world, but it seemed then the most miraculous."

"What date was that?"

"Back in 1860. Even I remember what a sensation this masterpiece created. It was designed by E. B. Dennison, afterward Lord Grimthorpe, and was placed one hundred and eighty feet above the ground—some halfway up the tower of one of the buildings. Now that fact in itself made the undertaking difficult, for the weather always has its effect on a clock, and to put one in such an exposed position created a problem at the outset. Moreover, perched up there in the sight of all London to serve as the chief timekeeper of the city, it could not be allowed to indulge in whims and caprices lest the populace be led astray by its inaccuracies and turn to cursing it. No, if it was to be there at all it must furnish correct information. Londoners could not afford to lose their trains, be late to their appointments, or miss their tea." The Scotchman uttered a soft laugh.

"Yes," continued he, as if the fancy pleased him, "when you are posted up in such a conspicuous spot as that, every one of your backslidings will be common property. And for that reason not only the reputation of the clock itself but that of its maker was at stake. Moreover, since the height at which the dial was to be set was so great, every part of the timepiece had to be of mammoth size."

"Of course it had," agreed Christopher. "I had almost forgotten that."

"A pretty gigantic project it was for a clockmaker, I can tell you," went on McPhearson. "Well, at last the clock was made and the scale of its dimensions sounded like a page from Gulliver's Travels. Each of the dials was of opalescent glass set in a framework of iron and was twenty-two feet or more in diameter. The figures that indicated the hours were two feet long and the minute spaces a foot square. Three sets of works were required to drive the various divisions of the mechanism: one moved the hands; another struck the hours; and still another rang the chimes. As for the pendulum—ah, here was a pendulum indeed! It was thirteen feet long and weighed seven hundred pounds."

"Jove!" murmured Christopher.

"Some pendulum, eh? What wouldn't the old clockmakers—Tompion, Quare, Fromanteel, Graham and the rest have given to see it! They probably never even imagined a clock of such proportions."

"Neither did I!" his companion announced. "How often did this giant have to be wound up?"

"The clock part was wound once a week; the striking part twice. And speaking of the striking part, you may like to know that the hour bell weighed thirteen tons and the four quarter-hour bells eight tons."

"Isn't it the biggest clock ever made?"

"It is probably one of the most powerful and most accurate of the large ones," nodded McPhearson, "although others are to be found with bigger dials. But it is no longer the largest clock in the world because since it was constructed several American rivals for that honor have arisen. One of them is right here in your own little old city of New York and the other is located on the New Jersey side of the Hudson River."

But Christopher's mind was still intent on the London masterpiece.

"How much do you suppose the English clock cost?" speculated he. "A fortune, I'll bet."

"I can tell you, for I happen to recall the figures," replied McPhearson. "Its price was $110,000."

"And cheap at that," grinned Christopher. "At least, I wouldn't undertake to produce it for that money."

"Nor I," echoed the Scotchman, returning the lad's smile. "I suppose when it was made nobody ever expected to see it equaled. And yet such strides are we making in science that here we are with a clock that is in many ways even more miraculous."

"You mean the one on the Metropolitan Life Insurance building?"

"The same," was the quick answer. "Surely you must grant that to be ahead of the one in London. It is interesting also to note how these two mammoth timepieces differ. The dial of our New York clock, instead of being of glass, is, as you know, of concrete faced with blue and white mosaic tiling. The figures indicating the hours are four feet high and the minute marks ten inches in diameter. The minute hands are twelve feet from center to tip and together weigh a thousand pounds; while the hour hands measure eight feet four inches from center to tip and weigh seven hundred pounds apiece."

"Mercy on us! I didn't realize it was such a whale of a thing!"

"*A prophet is not without honour save in his own country,*" laughed the old clockmaker. "Here you sit almost under the shadow of one of the largest timepieces in the universe and fail to appreciate the wonder that towers above your head. Well, well! Perhaps you will treat your native land with more respect after this. Certainly you will regard this Metropolitan Life clock with greater awe and bless your stars that one of its hands hasn't blown down on top of you. Think of those gigantic pointing fingers being built on iron frames sheathed with copper and made to revolve on roller bearings!"

"I give you my word I *shall* think of it the next time I look up at them," responded Christopher. "How on earth can they make such a tremendous machine go?"

"It is controlled automatically from the director's room, where a master clock also controls a hundred others scattered throughout the building. This same mechanism controls in addition various electrical devices, such as signal bells, etc. It is all very wonderful. And the half is not told yet, for the tricks it performs at night are almost more amazing than are those it performs by day."

"I seldom see it in the evening," Christopher explained. "We are always starting out into the suburbs just when New York is beginning to wake up."

"New York can hardly be called asleep at any time," McPhearson chuckled, "so I must take your lamentation with a grain of salt. But it is rather of a pity you shouldn't have had the chance to see that clock after dark. Not that it isn't beautiful in the daylight. Its chimes certainly ring just as sweetly one time as another.

Nevertheless I enjoy them best after the city gets a little bit quiet (which it seldom does until well toward morning). Those chimes, remember, are a replica of the set at Cambridge, England, and play a theme composed by Handel, the old composer."

"Why on earth didn't some one tell me all this before?"

"I'm sure I don't know, unless your dad was too busy or assumed you had read of the clock in the newspapers."

"It is never safe to assume I know anything," retorted Christopher naïvely. "I know such a queer collection of stuff, you see. It's odd, isn't it, the truck that sticks in your memory? If I could only remember things that are worth while as easily as I often do things that aren't I should know quite a lot".

"That is the way with all of us, laddie," the old man on the work bench confessed. "I myself would gladly part with a vast deal I have acquired and never yet found a use for."

"We ought to have mental rummage sales and bundle out the rubbish we don't need," Christopher remarked.

The Scotchman hailed the suggestion with delight.

"That would be a capital scheme," acclaimed he. "The only trouble would be to find purchasers for our outgrown ideas."

"Oh, somebody would like them," put in Christopher cheerfully. "Mother says there are always people who will buy anything that is cheap no matter what it is."

"But my old ideas are not cheap ones," objected the clockmaker. "On the contrary, some of them cost me a great deal in the day of them; they are simply worn out and old-fashioned."

"They'd sell—never fear. Mother declares people buy the most impossible truck. A thing is seldom so bad that nobody wants it."

"Then that is certainly what we must do with our intellectual junk," was McPhearson's instant answer. "Suppose we advertise a sale of it? I will cheerfully part with 'The Boy Stood on the

Burning Deck' which I committed to memory when I was eight years old. I'd sell it outright or would exchange it for one of Shakespeare's sonnets."

Christopher greeted the whimsey with a laugh.

"Now I," began he, "would sell or swap the water routes from most of our inland cities. We had to learn them when I studied geography and as I have never wanted to ship goods from St. Paul to Philadelphia, for example, I have found no use for them."

"You may some day."

"I'll risk it. If I did want them I could, perhaps, buy them back," flashed Christopher.

"What price would you set upon such possessions?"

"You mean the water routes? Well, it cost me a good deal of trouble to memorize them; still, I'd be glad to let them go cheap and be rid of them. I'd trade them for—let me see—an equal number of facts about wireless. With them I'd throw in all my—" he stopped suddenly.

"All your what?"

"I was going to say all my Latin but changed my mind," the boy replied. "I guess, everything considered, I'd better keep that. It might come in handy sometime. It did the other day."

"Oh, I'd keep your Latin, by all means," the Scotchman agreed.

A pause, weighted with humorous imaginings, fell between them until Christopher broke out:

"Mr. McPhearson!"

"Well?"

"How would you like to swap some more information about that clock on the Metropolitan Life building for my water routes?"

Gravely the clockmaker reflected.

"I'm afraid I haven't much more use for water routes just at present than you have," answered he. "I will, however, make a bargain with you. I will advance to you some more of what I know about that clock, if you will pledge yourself to let me have the water routes should I require them. Is that a bargain?"

"I'll sign up to that," came without hesitation from the lad. "In fact, after thinking it over, I guess it would be wiser for me not to agree to deliver the goods immediately. I'll have to hunt them up and—and—dust them first," concluded he with an impish grimace.

"I certainly should insist they be handed over in good condition," asserted McPhearson. "That would be only fair since what I give you in return is new and up to date. This clock on the insurance building is one of the most unique timepieces yet made. You cannot expect to receive information about it without offering something pretty valuable in exchange."

"No, indeed."

"That water route from St. Paul, for instance—I should never accept it if it began well and afterward became vague and uncertain; and should you break it off before you reached Philadelphia and excuse yourself by telling me that you had forgotten it—"

"You broke off about the clock, you know," interrupted Christopher.

"Yes. Nevertheless, I cannot be accused of having forgotten the information, and to prove it I will say that what I intended to add was that at night the numerals on the dial are not only illuminated but a flashlight from the tower sends out the time to those too far away either to see the face of the clock or hear it strike. A series of white flashes mark the hours, and the quarter hours are indicated by red flashes. Out over the land shoot these lights—out over the sea too. It is a mighty beacon—a great, throbbing, live thing that from its place high above the city keeps constant watch and slumbers not nor sleeps."

Christopher looked into the old man's eyes.

"I don't believe," ventured he, with a wistful expression, "it would be fair to swap any of the stuff I know for yours. You see, the things you have stored away in your mind are so much—so much finer."

"They weren't at first, laddie," returned McPhearson kindly. "I gathered a deal of worthless material before it occurred to me I could improve its quality. Then one day I said to myself, 'Why isn't it just as possible to collect beautiful and interesting thoughts as to collect stamps, or china teapots, or anything else?' So I set about weeding out the good from the unprofitable and found the scheme worked perfectly. If you don't believe it, try the plan yourself sometime, sonny."

"I'm going to," affirmed Christopher with earnest emphasis.

The Scotchman bent to file the tooth of a small brass wheel.

"Before we drop the subject of giant clocks," continued he presently, "I must warn you not to forget the monster newly set up by the Colgates on their building that skirts the Jersey shore of the Hudson. It is a veritable Titan with a dial fifty feet in diameter and hands measuring thirty-seven and a quarter feet and twenty-seven and a half feet in length. For miles down New York harbor it is visible, a formidable contestant for world supremacy."

"Clocks seem to grow bigger and bigger, don't they?" mused the boy.

"I hope they grow better and better—a far finer achievement, to my way of thinking," was the craftsman's answer.

CHAPTER XIII
CLOCKS ON LAND AND CLOCKS AT SEA

CHRISTMAS came and went, January passed, and February was well on its way, and still Christopher did not tire of coming into the city with his father each morning and spending the day at the store. He had found many little ways in which he could be useful and as a result he now had something to do to keep him from becoming bored and discontented. He could, for example, help deliver the sorted mail to the different departments and do various minor errands for McPhearson, toward whom he had come to entertain a genuine affection.

In the meantime he had been every week to see the oculist and each time had been commended for his patience and urged to be resigned to idleness a little longer.

"You'll gain in the end if you hold off until the year is out," said the doctor. "Remember, you have in all probability a long stretch of years ahead of you to the very last moment of which you will need your eyes. Therefore you cannot afford to injure them thus early in the game, for if you do you will never be able to beg, borrow, or steal another pair. What do a few short months amount to when weighed against a lifetime?"

It was a telling argument and immediately the lad sensed the worth of it.

"I figure you're right, Doctor Corbin," responded he bravely. "I'll peg away at being lazy for another spell. But don't keep me loafing any longer than you have to, will you? You see, just lately I have begun to be anxious to get back to my books. There are lots of things I want to hunt up and learn."

"Blessings brighten as they vanish, eh?" smiled the physician. "Well, it is something to have that impulse. Hold on to it; and when at last you have your books don't forget how fortunate you are to have them."

"I sha'n't—believe me!"

Accordingly Christopher gathered together his courage and as he himself expressed it *bucked up* to endure a prolonged period of inactivity. "I shall depend on you to cheer me up, Mr. McPhearson," announced he after recounting to the sympathetic Scotchman the doctor's decision. "If it weren't for you, I don't know what I'd do."

"Pooh! Nonsense! Non—*sense!* You'd find ways enough to amuse yourself without the help of an old fossil like me, I guess," blustered the clockmaker. Nevertheless it was plain to be seen the words pleased him, for he was a kind man who enjoyed doing a service for another. Moreover, Christopher had worn a path to his lonely heart and his boyish gladness transformed each day into a novelty to be anticipated.

Once when Mr. Burton had remained in the city to attend a dinner at the Lotus Club, McPhearson had persuaded his employer to allow the boy to go home with him and remain until the function was over. Ah, what an evening the two cronies had together that night! The Scotchman grilled chops in his tiny kitchenette and baked macaroni too; and made ambrosial hot chocolate. Then there were hot rolls, fancy cakes, and ice cream that appeared as it by magic from goodness only knew

AH, WHAT AN EVENING THE TWO CRONIES HAD TOGETHER THAT NIGHT.

where. And afterward, when the little flat had been tidied up (a task in which Christopher shared), McPhearson got out his flute and such wonderful old Scotch airs as he played! "Ye Banks and Braes o' Bonnie Doon," "Annie Laurie," "Mary of Argyle," "The Bonnets of Bonnie Dundee"—he knew them all and scores of others.

There was a fire in the microscopic fireplace, there was a box of candy, and there was plenty of fun and good talk. Later they had gone to see the big Metropolitan Life Insurance clock and watch its shooting red and white lights. Seldom had Christopher passed so happy an evening or one that flew by so quickly.

When Mr. Burton came with the taxi to take him home it was almost unbelievable it could really be eleven o'clock.

"I hope my son hasn't tired you all out, McPhearson," said the head of the firm. "It was very kind of you to bother with him."

"It was kind of you to let him come."

That was all the old man vouchsafed. He wasn't one given to talking much about the things he cherished deeply. But more than once after the boy had gone he recalled the picture the lad had made sitting there in the firelight; remembered the brightness of his smile and the gayety of his laughter. Even a flute could not furnish music as light-hearted. It was long since anything so joyous had echoed through the dim, dingy rooms. He wished he could fool himself into believing he was as young as he felt that night.

"Perhaps," observed he the next day, when Christopher referred to the evening, "your father will let you come again sometime. He may have another dinner or a meeting of some sort that will keep him in town."

"I wish he would," exclaimed Christopher heartily.

They were sitting together at the repairing bench, the clockmaker busy with an old chronometer.

"That's a new variety of puzzle, isn't it?" commented the boy, motioning toward it.

"Oh, I tinker a chronometer once in a while," McPhearson answered. "I don't get them often, though."

"What on earth are they for?"

"You don't know?" The Scotchman raised his brows with surprise.

"Not really. I associate them vaguely with the sea and ships."

"So far, so good," granted the elder man.

"But the trouble is that's as far as I can go," Christopher said.

"Bless me!" ejaculated McPhearson.

"I meant once to find out all about chronometers; but before I got started something interrupted me and I forgot it. I wasn't much interested in them anyhow, I'm afraid."

"And now you'd like a few points, eh?"

"Yes. I know I shall get a great deal better idea of them if you tell me," was the reply.

"If you weren't an American and I a Scotchman, I should say you were an Irishman," laughed his companion.

"Why?" demanded Christopher innocently.

"Because you sound as if you had kissed the Blarney Stone. Well, if you wish to learn about chronometers you have chosen a somewhat difficult subject. It leads pretty far, you see. However, I will do my best to give you at least a few facts about them. In the first place the earth actually revolves on its axis in twenty-three hours, fifty-six minutes, and four seconds. We commonly divide our day, however, into twenty-four hours and let it go at that. But astronomers reckon more accurately. They call our day the solar day and instead of having a clock with twelve figures on it as we do, they use one with twenty-four."

Christopher glanced up with a smile.

"Why be so fussy about things like minutes and seconds?"

"Because sometimes such things as minutes and seconds make a great deal of difference. You may remember that when we were talking of sundials I told you they were not exact timekeepers."

"I do remember."

"You see, we reckon our day by two counts: one of them begins at noon and goes on—one, two, three, four o'clock, etc.—up to midnight; the other begins at midnight and ends at noon."

"That's simple enough. I get that all right."

"Now people didn't always do that. There were other countries that planned their day differently. The ancient Babylonians, for instance, began their day at sunrise; the Athenians and Jews at sunset; and the Egyptians and Romans at midnight."

"How funny! I thought that of course it had always been done as we do it," confessed Christopher, with frank astonishment.

"Not at all. Our present system of time-keeping has been evolved out of the past and, like many other such heirlooms, is the result of a vast amount of study. Centuries ago nobody knew how to reckon time or what to reckon it by. Some computed it by the sun and had what is known as the solar day—a span of twenty-four hours; others figured it by the moon and got a lunar day of twenty-four hours and fifty minutes; while still others resorted to the stars or constellations and reached a result known as sidereal time, a day of twenty-three hours, fifty-six minutes. Now you see there is quite a bit of difference in these various reckonings. The difference might not matter so much on land, but when one is at sea and has to compute latitude and longitude, it matters a vast deal."

"Oh!" A light of understanding was slowly dawning on the boy.

"Now," went on McPhearson, "apparent solar time is dependent on the motion of the sun and is shown by the sundial; mean solar time, on the other hand, is shown by a correct clock; and the difference between the two—or the difference between apparent time and mean time is technically known as the equation of time, and is set forth in a nautical almanac published by the government."

McPhearson waited a moment.

"And that's what mariners use?"

"Yes."

"Then," hazarded Christopher after a moment's thought, "there really is exact time and common time."

"Broadly speaking, yes," acquiesced McPhearson. "Or in other words there is time scientifically measured and time that is measured by man-made laws. The difference, as I told you, is of more importance to astronomers and mariners than to anybody else; and yet the puzzle for many centuries balked those who sought to establish a perfect system of time-keeping. As better ships were built and adventurous persons began to sail the ocean both for trade and conquest, captains soon discovered the stars and the compass could not be relied upon to furnish them the reliable information they needed in locating their position. Therefore, about 1713 England offered a prize of £20,000 to any one who should invent a timekeeper sufficiently accurate to enable navigators to ascertain from it longitude at sea."

The Scotchman paused to take from his table a box of tiny brass screws from which he selected one that was to his liking.

"Now there was living at this period John Harrison, a Yorkshire clockmaker, who although quite a young man had made a clock with wooden works into which he had put a gridiron pendulum—a device he had thought out to overcome the difficulties resulting from atmospheric conditions. This clock was so skillfully adjusted that it did not vary a second a month. So you can see that despite the fact Harrison was not a member of the Clockmakers' Company he was certainly qualified to be."

"And did he go after the prize money?"

"Apparently the offer tempted him. Perhaps he not only desired to win the fortune offered but also wished the fun of solving the riddle the government propounded. At any rate, in 1728 he came to London prepared to present drawings of an instrument he felt certain would turn the trick and had not his friends deterred him he would have placed these sketches before the commission. Fortunately, however, he had excellent advisers (among whom was honest John Graham) and they assured him he would stand a far better chance of securing a favorable hearing should he first construct the instrument of which he at present had nothing but pictures. Now such counsel as this was pretty disheartening to a young man who, fired with hope and ambition, had come all the way to London confidently expecting to have his plan hailed with joy when he arrived. Nevertheless Harrison was open-minded enough to accept his friends' guidance and acting upon it he went home again and worked for seven years on the instrument he had drawn out on paper."

"And then did he bring it to London?" was Christopher's breathless demand.

"Yes," affirmed McPhearson. "The contrivance, however, was by no means perfect. Still it showed sufficient promise to interest the commissioners and lead them to give Harrison permission to go to Lisbon on one of the king's ships; that he might correct his reckonings by taking practical observations at sea. Moreover they also paid him £5,000 of the prize money to encourage him. This financial spur, together with the faith it represented, stimulated the patient instrument-maker to fashion a second timekeeper on which he spent four years of hard work. But even this one, although better than the first, failed to meet the demands, and he tried again, taking ten years to perfect a third. This was smaller and as it seemed to foreshadow good results he was awarded the gold medal annually presented by the Royal Society for the most useful nautical discovery thus far made. Yet notwithstanding this triumph the article he had produced did not suit him. Experience had, in the meantime, taught him a great deal, and after more corrections and improvements he came again before the committee and asked that the device he now had might be given practical trial."

Christopher hitched his stool a little nearer.

"Now governments, like elephants and mastodons, move slowly, and by the time the coveted permission was granted poor Harrison was well-nigh seventy years old and instead of setting out on an ocean voyage for Jamaica he was forced to surrender his place to his son, William, whom he had trained up as one of his apprentices."

"Poor old duffer! I'll bet he was disappointed," came sympathetically from Christopher. "Think of his having to stay at home and miss the fun of seeing how his invention was working!"

"It was pretty tough," agreed McPhearson. "William, in the meantime, sailed out of Portsmouth harbor and after eighteen days of voyaging the vessel, supposed by ordinary calculation to be 13° 50' west of that port, was by Harrison's watch 15° 19', whereupon the captain of the ship immediately cried that it was worthless. If William had not been a chip of the old block and had inherited some of his father's courage, wisdom, and persistence, he would have lost his nerve at this crisis and allowed himself to come home beaten. But evidently he believed in the venture he had in hand. Perhaps, too, the thought of how disappointed his poor old dad would be were he to return spurred him to hold on with bulldog tenacity. So instead of being cowed by this apparent failure he insisted that if Madeira were correctly charted on the captain's map, it would be sighted the next day. So convincing was his prediction that the reluctant officer at length consented to continue on his course, and sure enough the following morning there loomed Madeira just as William had prophesied! Having won out on this forecast, William kept on predicting just where the other islands would be and behold, one after another they came into sight!"

"Hurray!" cried Christopher.

"Well, after a trip of sixty-one days the *Deptford* reached Port Royal, and the chronometer (for that is what this new sort of watch really was) proved to be only about nine seconds slow. Then followed the voyage home. William Harrison had been gone five months in all—five months which to his poor, anxious old father must have seemed five years in length. During that entire time the chronometer had varied only one minute and five seconds."

"Pooh! That wasn't anything to get hot over," exploded Christopher.

"And yet a variation as great as that represented an error of eighteen miles—a big enough distance to admit of a ship being run on no end of rocks and shoals."

"I didn't realize it amounted to so many miles," was the sober reply.

"Probably the error even in miles did not shock people of that time as much as it would us, for they were accustomed to inaccuracies. Moreover such a record was worlds better than anything previously known. Yet notwithstanding this fact, the commissioners haggled over awarding the prize money and after advancing another £5,000 insisted that William make a second trip."

"Shucks!"

McPhearson paid no heed to the interruption.

"This time," continued he, "the undaunted young clockmaker embarked on an English man-of-war, the *Tartar*, and sailed for the Barbados, the chronometer gaining only forty-three seconds; and then back he came on the *New Elizabeth*, making the round trip of one hundred fifty-six days with only a total gain of fifty-four seconds in his father's instrument."

"Bravo! And so old Harrison at last got his money," asserted Christopher with a satisfied sigh.

"Not yet. You move too fast, sonny. Governments do not bestow fortunes at your pace. Not they! This time the commissioners paid over a third £5,000, joining with it the demand that the elder Harrison explain to a company of experts exactly how his invention worked. In our day a man would have protected himself with a patent before he surrendered the requested information but the universe of the eighteenth century was less sophisticated. Patiently Harrison told his inquisitors everything they wanted to know and in 1765 they declared themselves satisfied with the instrument in every detail."

"Well, I should think it was high time!" scoffed the boy.

The Scotchman smiled at his indignation.

"Oh, don't imagine yourself through with the story yet," said he, "for even now more conditions were enjoined. Before the balance of the prize money was paid, one of the experts was appointed to construct a chronometer like Harrison's for the purpose not only of finding out whether every claim he made for it was true, but also to assure the board that other persons beside this one old man could make such an instrument. The fulfillment of this final condition consumed three years."

"Oh, rats! I should have told them they could keep their money—the old grannies!" jeered his listener wrathfully.

"They had to be sure, you know."

"But poor Harrison! What was he doing in the meantime?"

"Growing to be a very old man, alas!" McPhearson answered in a saddened voice. "It was not until 1773 that the last of the £20,000 for which he had so valiantly struggled was given him."

"I'm thankful he got it and hadn't died."

"He died three years later—an old man of eighty-three. Nevertheless he lived long enough to see his dream fulfilled. Sixty years of his life he had devoted to experimenting with and perfecting his chronometer. It was a great service to the world—a deed that influenced not only all subsequent clockmaking but ultimately all marine enterprises. It also, by making navigation easier, saved innumerable lives. Other scientists followed and built on his discoveries until now, thanks to them all, the sea is practically as safe and familiar a spot to dwell upon as is the land. No longer are vessels at a loss to know where they are. With the finely adjusted nautical instruments at their command, scientific books, wireless communication, and the correct time sent out each day by radio they have no excuse for failing to make and maintain accurate observations."

"But poor old Harrison—I cannot help regretting he had to wait so long for his prize money," bewailed Christopher.

"I rather think, laddie, had you asked the inventor of the chronometer which gave him the greater satisfaction—the award the English Government paid him or the joy derived from successfully working out the puzzle it propounded—he would have told you that in his estimation, when weighed the one against the other, the money counted for nothing—nothing!"

CHAPTER XIV
HOW RUBIES, SAPPHIRES, AND GARNETS HELPED TO TELL TIME

WELL, Christopher, what do you think of the jewelry business?" his father inquired one day after he had been for several months a regular visitor at the store.

Christopher smiled.

"I like parts of it very much," replied he. "The clocks and watches are all right. There's sense in those. I shouldn't mind a bit becoming a repairer if I could be as good a one as Mr. McPhearson. But the rings, bracelets and all those ruby-emerald-diamond fol-de-rols make me sick."

"And yet you could have no fine watches without jewels—remember that."

Abashed, the lad colored.

"Oh, I know the best watches have their works dolled up with precious stones."

"Scarcely *dolled up*, son," Mr. Burton answered.

"I thought that was what they were put in for."

"Just for ornament?"

"Sure! To make the watches handsomer than those carried by common folks—dressier and more expensive."

"You actually entertained that notion?" came quizzically from the head of the firm.

"Yes, Dad."

Mr. Burton gazed at his offspring dumbfounded and reproachful, his eyes saying as plainly as any words could, "That I should live to hear a son of mine give voice to such gross ignorance!" Then when he had conquered his amazement sufficiently to speak he gasped:

"I'm afraid there are still facts that McPhearson will have to teach you before you can follow his trade."

"No doubt there are a few," returned Christopher audaciously.

"This matter of jeweled watches is one. How did it happen you never asked him why precious stones were set in the works of a watch?"

"I thought I knew why."

"He probably thought you did too; but apparently you don't. However, there is hope for you since you are willing to be honest and confess your ignorance. Indeed, I've no right to blame you. How should you know such a thing unless somebody took the trouble to tell you?" the lad's father amended. "Nevertheless, at first I could not but be surprised at the originality of your theory."

"Then the jewels are not for decoration?"

"Well, hardly!" responded Burton, Senior, with an amused shake of his head. "Way back about the year 1700 a Genevan watchmaker residing in London struggled to find some hard material in which to set watch pivots so they would not wear the works of the watch, and after much experimenting with different substances he hit upon the plan of drilling a hole in various kinds of gems and setting the pivots into those. Gems, as perhaps you are already aware, are among the hardest minerals we have. Therefore Facio, as the Swiss was called, proceeded to make a watch after this idea and in 1703 obtained a patent on it good for fourteen years. Then, two years later, when he found by experience how excellent and practical was his scheme, he petitioned that this grant be extended to cover a longer period.

"Now all workmen, alas, are jealous for their own prestige and the artisans belonging to the London Clockmakers' Company were no exception to this rule. All of them were ready enough to seize greedily upon the bright ideas of any craftsman following their line of trade and they resented it bitterly if not allowed to do so. Moreover, that it was Nicolas Facio, a Swiss, and not one of their own number who had stumbled upon this clever device was galling indeed. Therefore, I regret to say, they opposed his application for the extending of his patent on the ground that the jewel idea was not new. A member of their own guild, they insisted, had already constructed such a watch; and to prove the assertion they produced a timepiece with an amethyst gleaming from its works. Upon the presentation of this evidence the unlucky Facio's claim was immediately refused. Later on, however, it proved that the watch displayed by the zealous London gentlemen was not in the least similar to Facio's conception. The jewel had only been stuck on (in accordance with your own plan) and was not set into the works at all. Whether the fraud resulted from ignorance or was a deliberate attempt to deceive no one could say. Certainly in 1703 the London clockmakers had nothing with which to block Facio's application; if, therefore, in 1705 they had a jeweled watch, it looks much as if they must have deliberately prepared it as an argument against the Genevan's request being granted. What the facts were we shall probably never know; but at least poor Facio lost the glory due him for his invention. Since that time practically all watches have certain of their moving parts set in jewels to prevent wear to the bearings and make them run smoother. The more expensive watches contain many of these stones. It requires less power, you see, to drive a well-jeweled watch because of its velvet-like action. But at the same time all this studding of gems greatly increases the cost of making a good watch."

"What a duffer I was to think the jewels were just to make the thing look pretty!" burst out Christopher, when his father had finished.

"Don't come down on yourself too hard, son," Mr. Burton interposed kindly. "We all have to learn. But you can now understand, can't you, that the diamonds, rubies, and precious stones at which you jeered have their practical uses? A pivot or bearing revolving in a hole drilled in a garnet or other gem creates almost no friction and needs therefore only very little oil."

"I can understand it now—yes, sir," returned Christopher meekly.

"Of course in our day the price of jewels has gone up a great deal. There was a time when a full-jeweled watch did not begin to cost what it does now. However, we are free of certain other expenses the old watchmakers encountered," went on Mr. Burton. "For example, about the year 1800, when England was anxious to raise money for the treasury, William Pitt proposed that a tax be placed on the wearing of watches."

"That's worse than having to pay a tax on theater tickets—a good sight!" jested Christopher.

"It certainly meant the taxation of a very useful commodity; we should term it an indispensable one. At that period of history, though, watches and clocks were far less cheap and common and therefore Mr. Pitt may have classed them as luxuries and rated them as our government does perfumery. However that may be, his suggestion of levying two shillings sixpence on every silver watch and ten shillings on every gold one, with the additional tax of five shillings on every clock, went through."

"I don't see why the English people stood for it," said the boy, his hereditary resentment against unjust taxation aroused.

"They were pretty thoroughly vexed, I assure you," was the reply. "It meant, you see, very disastrous results for the horologists. In fact, even outside the trade feeling ran high. Not only were numberless excellent workmen thrown out of their jobs and the watchmaking industry given a general setback, but the public, just coming to appreciate the value of a good timepiece, was vastly inconvenienced. Many persons revolted and ceased to carry watches rather than pay the tax. Some did this as a protest; others because they could not afford the additional expenditure. In the meantime an article known as the Act of Parliament clock was made and put up in the taverns, inns, and coffee houses to aid customers and serve as an additional declaration against the Pitt tax. So general was public disapproval and so bitter the storm created that a year after the law had passed it had to be repealed."

"That's the stuff! It ought to have been," cried young America fervently.

"Yes, I agree with you. It certainly was a mistaken method for raising an income for the State. Once abolished, the industry slowly began to pick up again. Nevertheless, for all that, England never thrived at watchmaking as did France, Switzerland and our own nation. One reason was because she clung stubbornly to the old-fashioned fusee long after other people had abandoned it for the spring. There she made a great mistake. Still, after this Pitt tax was abolished, the craft began, as I said, to get on its feet again. Little by little machinery replaced hand labor and as more watches were turned out the price of them dropped. Also, as foreign trade increased, it became possible to import from other countries parts or the entire works of both clocks and watches. Perhaps had not this arrangement been so easy and simple, England would have been obliged to buck up and evolve a big watch industry of her own; as it was she followed the less difficult path and never went into the manufacture on a large scale with factories and all that."

"How about the French?" Christopher inquired.

"The French, no one can deny, were very ingenious watch-makers. To begin with, they had artistic ideas and great cleverness in producing beautiful and unique designs. The wrist watch, held by thousands of people to be such a boon, was of French invention. But it was the Swiss who were the master watchmakers of the Old World. A French horologer moved to Switzerland, carrying his trade with him, and as a result there soon grew up in Geneva a guild of workmen not to be outranked. There had been watchmakers there before, but the standards this guild created established a quality of work hitherto unknown. Men learned their trade and excelled in it until every part of a Swiss watch, one might almost say, was turned out by an expert. Some artisans made nothing but small wheels, some large ones; some fashioned pivots, some drilled jewels in which to set them. Afterward the watch was assembled, as we call it—all its parts being gathered together, put in place, and adjusted. A Geneva watch thus constructed bore what was practically the trademark of excellence. There was nothing finer on the market."

"Were all Swiss watches equally good?" inquired Christopher.

"As a general thing a Swiss watch could be depended on. However, different cities differed in output. None of them maintained the high standard Geneva established, although Neuchatel, its closest rival, made a great many fine and beautiful watches. In other centers, too, the trade was carried on successfully. But it remained for our own country to develop a vast factory system where every part of a watch was constructed beneath one roof. This innovation, together with the fact that eventually watches came to be made on regulation scales with interchangeable parts, greatly bettered as well as increased watch production."

"I've quite a curiosity to know how this big factory system and in fact the whole clock and watch industry got started in America," the boy observed.

His father smiled.

"That," replied he, "is, as Kipling says, another story, and a long one too. I don't know that I myself could follow every step of it. But you will find McPhearson can. So seriously has he taken his profession that he is not to be floored by anything in time-keeping history. Ask him to tell you what you wish to know."

"He does seem to be mighty well up in his trade, doesn't he?" acknowledged the boy, pleased to hear this tribute to his friend. "He has collected quite a few interesting things related to it, too. The night I was there he showed me a lot of old watch papers he has been years picking up. He told me that long ago, when watches were thicker than they are now, there was a space left between the covers and inside it people put all sorts of things—pictures, small designs embroidered or painted on satin, mottoes, figures pricked on paper until they made raised patterns, poems, and portraits."

"So McPhearson has some of those, has he? Well, well! Some-time I must ask him about them," Mr. Burton said. "The custom of carrying such souvenirs was quite common in England at the time. If a man owned a fine ship or was interested in one, he had a small picture of her painted to put inside the cover of his watch; or he carried a likeness of his wife or sweetheart there. Sometimes, on the other hand, he was patriotically inclined and chose to devote this cherished space to a picture of the king or some national idol. Or maybe he was of literary bent and gave over the shrine to a religious text, a love poem, a maxim, or a moral admonition that he wished to keep daily before him. Even we ourselves often paste pictures in our watches. We have never, however, gone into the craze as the English of this particular era did. With them it was a fashionable fad that resulted in all manner of curious conceits. They had no kodaks, you see, and small pictures were rarer possessions then than now." Mr. Burton paused a moment to puff little rings of smoke thoughtfully into the air. "So McPhearson has made a collection of those old watch-papers, has he!" mused he. "Maybe he would loan them to us and let us exhibit them here at the store sometime. They are quite rare now and would be interesting."

"I think he would be tremendously pleased to do so, Dad," responded Christopher. "He is far too modest ever to suggest doing it himself."

"Oh, we should never know it if McPhearson had the Kohi-noor right in his pocket. He would be the last person in the world to tell of it," laughed Mr. Burton. "I know what he is. I am also well aware that he has been very kind to you during these past few months. When the time comes right, I mean to let him know that I have not been blind to his interest and generosity."

"I'd like above everything else to give him a—well, some sort of present when my eyes—*if* my eyes ever get well again," faltered Christopher a trifle uncertainly.

"Come, come, son! You mustn't talk in that strain," objected Mr. Burton, noticing the depression in the boy's tone. "Of course your eyes are coming out all right. Aren't they worlds better already?"

The lad sighed.

"The doctor says they are," replied he wearily.

"Then what are you fussing about?" blustered Burton, Senior. "You've no cause to be downhearted, my son. Why, when you get back to school you will bound ahead like a trooper. You will find that in a few months you will make up all you've lost—see if you don't; and I believe you will enjoy studying, too, after being so long deprived of books."

"I know I shall see more sense in doing it than I ever did before," asserted Christopher with earnestness. "Somehow, since I've talked so much with Mr. McPhearson, learning things seems more worthwhile."

"You like the old Scotchman, don't you?"

"He's a brick!"

"Then you wouldn't consider it a hardship to be in his company for a while?"

"How—*in his company?*" asked the boy, glancing up quickly in puzzled surprise.

"Oh, I don't know," was the vague retort.

Nevertheless, as Mr. Burton turned his eyes away, Christopher noticed his father was smiling the meditative, enigmatic smile that he smiled once in a blue moon. It was usually when some particularly delightful reverie occupied his mind that his face took on that especial expression. The lad wondered what he was thinking about this time.

CHAPTER XV
CLOCKS IN AMERICA

"S AY, Mr. McPhearson, I wish you would tell me how clocks got to America," demanded Christopher when he and the old Scotchman were next together. "Of course the Pilgrim Fathers couldn't have brought them all."

The watchmaker chuckled.

"To hear folks boast about their ancestral possessions you would think the *Mayflower* might also have brought a few hundred clocks in addition to all the bales of china, tables, chairs, and beds she is credited with transporting," replied he. "In point of fact, however, clocks did not reach these shores by any such romantic method. The early clockmakers came over here from England and Holland precisely as did other adventurous craftsmen. Often they were by trade gold or silversmiths who combined with other arts that of making clocks. As a result, while some of them were skilled horologers others merely turned out clocks as a side issue."

"Most likely the people over here were thankful to get any clocks at all," the boy ventured.

"Evidently there were clockmakers who worked on that theory," was McPhearson's dry answer. "Do not imagine, however, that I am condemning wholesale all the early clockmakers. On the contrary there were among them many really good workmen and every now and then a clock crops up that testifies to the skill of its dead-and-gone creator. Number Seventeen, for example, that you saw at Mr. Hawley's, was such a one. It was made, you remember, by John Bailey of Hanover, Massachusetts, and ever since the close of the eighteenth century it has ticked faithfully on, keeping excellent time. What more can you ask of a clock than that? And that is only one of many. Had we a complete list of all those early American makers, how interesting it would be! But, alas, they landed and scattered over the country, settling here and settling there, and with a few exceptions we can trace them only through town records. Two that have been successfully tracked down are William Davis, recorded as being in Boston in 1683; and Everardus Bogardus, who was located in New York in 1698. Also in 1707 there is mention of a James Patterson arriving from London and opening a Boston shop. Probably John Bailey, who was no doubt one of the clockmaking Baileys of Yorkshire, was a pioneer of a little later period. We can only list these men as we stumble upon their handiwork. Unfortunately, there are early clocks whose makers it is impossible to trace. A good many such timepieces were made for the interiors of churches or for their steeples. The church at Ipswich, Massachusetts, built in 1699, which at first had only a bell to mark the hours, arrived five years later at the dignity of a clock having both face and hands."

"That sounds like the old days in England," exclaimed Christopher.

"It was a turn backward," conceded McPhearson. "For a time our American clock history repeats in part the history of the race. We did not, to be sure, revert to water clocks; but our forefathers did not scorn to resort to sundials, sand glasses, and noon marks. And even after clocks made their appearance in this country they were at first very sparsely distributed. Many an amusing incident concerning them is found in the annals of various towns.

"New Haven as early as 1727 put up a modest little church and in 1740 decided to dignify it with a clock and bell. Accordingly Ebenezer Parmilee constructed for the parish a clock with brass works which the committee agreed to *try*. Fancy his amazement when the trial of his handiwork dragged on for two long years! The people had been keen to get the clock but having once secured it they were not, I fear, equally keen about paying for it. History relates that two of the congregation who had previously pledged themselves to shoulder a portion of the expense backed out when the final settlement was imminent, on the plea that they lived too far away either to see the clock or hear it strike."

"They were squealers all right!" derided his listener.

McPhearson turned on him with twinkling eyes.

"Listen to the sequel," continued he. "In 1825 it was decided to have a second clock put up—one that would do better under the varying weather conditions—and a bargain was struck with Barzillai Davidson to take over the old clock, allowing forty dollars for its brass works; and set up in its place one with wooden works costing about three hundred dollars. This Mr. Davidson agreed to do. He therefore made the new clock, put it up, and then departed, carrying with him all the brass wheels, pivots and things the thrifty Ipswich fathers had discarded. Imagine if you can the chagrin of these worthies when later they heard that the canny clockmaker had reassembled the brass works they had bartered off and converted them into a timepiece which he forthwith sold in New York for six hundred dollars!"

"That certainly was one on the town fathers," replied the lad, greeting the story with ringing laughter.

"The saying goes that one has to get up in the morning to beat a Yankee or a Scotchman at a bargain," was McPhearson's quiet observation. "I could add to this tale many another one of the early clockmakers. They were ingenious old fellows. Indeed, they had to be. Some of them, to be sure, brought tools with them from England; but at best there were only a few such articles to be purchased even on the other side of the water where every type of machinery was scarce and still in its infancy. Therefore the majority of workmen had to fashion their own implements and make their clocks with only a hammer, file, and drill to help them. When you consider that, it is little short of a miracle they were able to produce articles that would keep time with even a reasonable degree of accuracy. But they contrived to—oh, yes, indeed! Of course they did not reach their best results immediately. It took a while. Still as clocks continued to make their appearance the product generally became better and better. An excellent one, put up in a church steeple in Newburyport in 1786, was made by Simon Willard, a great Massachusetts clockmaker of whom I will sometime tell you more. There was also a clock of Boston make on the Old South Meeting House sometime before 1768; and Gawen Brown, who made it, also made a long-case clock for the Massachusetts State House. There were good clockmakers in both New York and Philadelphia by the year 1750. So, you see, it was quite possible to buy either a watch or a clock fairly early in our colonial history."

"What type of clock did such makers turn out?" was Christopher's interrogation.

"For use in the homes the long-case clock was the style favored," McPhearson responded. "Some of these had brass works and seconds pendulums and ran eight days, and others were thirty-hour clocks with works of wood. Nevertheless, although they were to be had, they were still something of a luxury and every one did not possess the money to purchase them; nor, indeed, were they held to be indispensable, many of the more conservative families preferring still to use the hourglass even as late as 1812."

"That was the year of the war, wasn't it?" the lad hazarded.

"Yes. The colonists had already had the Revolution on their hands and national affairs were in such a turmoil it was difficult for any one to put his mind on building up a trade. But after a while life calmed down into more tranquil grooves and then clockmaking, like other occupations, leaped into prosperity. New England, where many of the first clockmakers had originally settled, led the country in this industry as was natural she should, more improvements and inventions being perfected there than anywhere else. And Connecticut was the banner State. She boasted a large group of successful makers, any one of whom was a master at his craft. The names of some of them are Daniel Burnap, Thomas Harland, Eli Terry, Eli Terry, Junior, Silas Hoadley, Seth Thomas, and Chauncey Jerome. Harland was an expert from London and had a hand in training a goodly number of American apprentices, among whom the elder Terry was one. The career of the latter man reads like a fairy tale. In common with other early workers he labored at the disadvantage of having few tools. He may, perhaps, have owned a hand engine of the sort used in England at the period, but until he bethought him of using water power he had little else to aid him."

"Did he make the long-case clock, too?" asked Christopher.

"Yes. That style of clock, you see, provided space for a lengthy, slow-swinging pendulum. Nevertheless although it was a popular variety, it was anything but a convenient one to handle, being both bulky and awkward to transport. For this reason many such clocks were sold without cases—a custom borrowed from England—it being understood that buyers should furnish cases of their own. Only too often, alas, this part of the contract was never carried out and the unfortunate *wag-on-the-wall* (as this sort of timepiece was eventually dubbed) was hung up all unprotected from dust and dampness."

"Do you mean to say they really christened clocks by that unearthly name?" asked Christopher incredulously.

"*Wag-on-the-wall?* Yes, indeed. That was the term they went by. Pedlars carried them round on horseback, riding from house to house and jolting them over the bad roads until it is a seven-days' wonder they went at all," was McPhearson's retort.

"I never saw a clock of the sort," the lad mused.

"They are rare now. I suppose most of them were discarded years ago. You see, since they had no cases they probably became clogged with dirt and wore out much sooner than did the protected long-case clocks; moreover, as they were both cheap and commonplace, nobody thought of keeping them after something better was procurable. Who would dream of laying them aside and cherishing them because they might in years to come be curiosities of historic value? Americans never keep anything, you know. It is a seven-days' wonder how they ever chanced to possess any heirlooms at all."

Christopher smiled at the Scotchman's savage grumble.

"Thomas Harland made quite a few of these wags-on-the-wall as well as some fine long-case clocks with works of brass," added the old man.

"I suppose none of the makers could turn out very many

clocks when every part of them had to be made by hand," was Christopher's thoughtful comment.

"No, they couldn't. Moreover the demand for clocks was not great. Usually clockmakers either started only three or four or else began none until they received advance orders. If eight or ten good clocks that would sell for thirty-five or forty dollars apiece were turned out inside a year, the output was held to be a pretty fair one."

"Nobody could get very rich on that income," came from the lad.

"Not if that rate of production had continued. But it didn't, you see. After Eli Terry got to making clocks somewhere about 1795 he was clever enough to carry water from a near-by brook into his shop and supplement his tools and hand engine with water power. That was a stride ahead of the old way and opened before him all manner of undreamed-of possibilities, as a result of which he decided to make clocks on a tremendous scale. The type of thing he aimed to produce was a thirty-hour clock with wooden works and a pendulum vibrating seconds; and he figured that by purchasing more water power and larger buildings he would be able to make such clocks at the rate of a thousand or more a year and therefore turn them out for as little as four dollars apiece—a mad enterprise in that era of limited economic conditions."

"Did the scheme make good?"

"Not to the extent he had hoped," answered McPhearson. "He could, it is true, make clocks with wooden works much cheaper than with works of brass; but he did not feel satisfied with them and after the year was up he abandoned the venture. Hence this variety of clock of the elder Terry workmanship is rarely to be found. A somewhat crude timepiece it was, having no dial and only figures painted on the glass at the front of the case to indicate the hours. Peering through it one could see the works. But although Eli Terry himself gave up making this style of clock, others who had caught his idea did not and consequently a good many of them came into the market. In fact most of Terry's inspirations were thanklessly snatched up by his contemporaries, for in all his years of work he took out only one patent."

A protest escaped Christopher's lips.

"Patents were held in no very high esteem in those days," continued McPhearson. "People did not regard them in the light we do now. You remember how the old clockmakers of London blocked the path whenever a member of their craft attempted to secure one. They wished to share the benefits of everybody's ideas and therefore maintained that all inventions should be common property. As a rule those who clamored most loudly that this altruistic arrangement be promoted were those who never had any brilliant ideas of their own. As for the inventors themselves—they were as a rule too intent on the thing they were producing to pay any great heed to the money end of the project. Eli Terry was a man of this character. Therefore it came about that when others copied the circular saw he installed and made off with the other fruits of his brain he raised no protest."

"Did he never make any more clocks with wooden works?" inquired Christopher.

"Oh, yes, indeed! By 1814 he had worked out a fresh model of a wooden clock that he liked much better than his first. This one vibrated half-seconds and accordingly could be made with a pendulum short enough for the timepiece to be placed on a shelf as the former one had been. It was, however, of an entirely new design, having a dial in the upper half, painted glass in the door and an ornamental pillar at each side of the case. On top was a decorative scroll of wood and altogether it was a product so novel and well suited to the home that immediately the public greeted it with delight."

"And I suppose all the other clockmakers promptly began to copy it," interposed Christopher.

"Precisely!" smiled the Scotchman. "The old wag-on-the-wall, and in many instances even the grandfather clock was consigned to the ash heap, and the pillar clock became the only clock worth having. It was, fortunately, within range of the most modest purse, costing only fifteen dollars. Mr. Terry now had more business than he could handle and he took in his two sons, Henry and Eli, Junior, to learn the trade and help him. Of course this wonderful commodity could not be imported because if taken to sea the dampness would swell its wooden wheels and ruin it. Nevertheless Terry did not care. He had all the trade he could manage right here at home. For twenty-five years his wooden clocks remained in vogue, a long period to hold the favor of the fickle public. Great credit is due Mr. Terry, too, for bringing such a clock into being, for a timepiece with wooden works meant the making of an entirely different set of tools, since it was impossible to use the same implements that were required in the making of clocks with works of brass."

"I suppose it was a change in fashion that finally caused the downfall of the wooden-wheeled clock," was Christopher's comment.

He ventured the remark with some pride.

"No, in this particular case it wasn't. Capricious as fashion is, people liked the shelf clock much better than they did a tall clock that stood on the floor, and they would no doubt have continued to buy these clocks with wooden works had not sheet metal began to be manufactured about the year 1840. Instantly clockmakers saw the advantage of having sheet brass to work with. It was far better than the cast brass formerly used. An improvement, too, were the wire pinions—accessories much cheaper and simpler to produce than were those of wood. Therefore just as wood forced the old cast brass out of favor, so sheet brass now took the place of wood. Fortunately for Eli Terry, the drastic changes he had instituted in the fashioning of his clocks were equally possible of manufacture either from cast or sheet material."

"No doubt by that time the whole country had gobbled up his inventions," sniffed Christopher.

"Yes. The best of his ideas had been seized and generally put into practice not only on this side of the ocean but also on the other. Two of his ideas were everywhere popular—the placing of the dial works between plates; and the mounting of the verge on a small steel pin inserted in one end of the short arm. But in spite of all the improvements he had made, Mr. Terry did not sit down with folded hands and feel there was nothing further to be done. Constantly he was alert for practical suggestions that should better his handiwork. For example, he heard that some one was making machinery according to a definite scale so that parts of it could be exchanged from one article to another. Why, thought he, should not the parts of a clock be made so they would be interchangeable? The plan proved a most excellent one and eventually it was universally adopted by other clockmakers. So you see, in one way and another, old Eli Terry contributed very materially to up-building the American clockmaking industry."

"Did his sons go on making clocks?" was Christopher's inquiry.

"Yes," nodded McPhearson. "In fact, ever so many clockmaking Terrys came after old Eli, and each added his bit to his ancestor's trade. One branched out and made tempered steel clock springs to take the place of the expensive springs of brass which were too costly to put into the cheaper grade of American-made clocks. Oh, yes, the Terrys kept up the traditions of the family—never fear about that! All that group of early Connecticut manufacturers did great service to the country in founding an industry that has brought to the United States a goodly portion of its business prosperity. Seth Thomas, Silas Hoadley, Chauncey Jerome are names that will not soon be forgotten; Terryville and Thomaston, two clockmaking centers, testify to that. As for Jerome—it was he who experimented with the painting of decorative glass and evolved that variety having a bronzed effect."

"Oh, I know what you mean," interrupted Christopher with quick intelligence. "Our kitchen clock has glass like that in the door. And meantime, while Connecticut was doing so much, what were the other states up to?"

"Let me think a moment," replied the Scotchman, half closing his eyes. "Well, Rhode Island never furnished much aid along the line of clockmaking; her talents seemed to lie in the direction of spinning yarn, making thread, and weaving textiles. What clocks she needed were imported or made by hand by local silversmiths. Pennsylvania, however, contributed her part. David Rittenhouse of Philadelphia was an exceedingly skillful clockmaker who not only had to his credit many fine timepieces but also some very complicated and remarkable ones. Christopher Sower, too, was a Pennsylvania man not to be overlooked."

"Christopher, eh?" the boy repeated.

"Yes. There are some exceedingly distinguished Christophers in history, remember. You and Columbus are not the only ones," asserted McPhearson, with dancing eyes. "This Christopher Sower, now, could turn not alone his hand but his well-trained brain in a variety of worthy directions. To begin with, before he settled in Germantown he had taken a doctor's degree in an Old World medical university. Therefore after becoming established on his American farm he not only tilled the land but he doctored his neighbors. In addition he took up clockmaking, paper-making, and the printing of books. And as if these vocations, or avocations, did not keep him busy enough, he supplemented them by trying to improve the manufacture of cast-iron stoves. Even he himself, perhaps, felt it necessary to offer apology for dabbling in so many trades, for when he came to put his name on his clocks he spelled it *Souers*."

The lad smiled.

"Then there was also in Pennsylvania a friend of Benjamin Franklin's, Edward Duffield, who made good clocks. Meantime in New Hampshire both Timothy Chandler of Concord and Luther Smith of Keene were successfully plying the clockmaking trade and creating beautiful old clocks. But it was Massachusetts that was Connecticut's strong second."

"And what was being done there?"

McPhearson put down his drill.

"Were I to begin that story," protested he, "I should have no lunch to-day and you would have none either. Maybe some other time—"

"To-morrow?" suggested Christopher, who had no intention of allowing this prince of story-tellers to escape.

"Why, yes—to-morrow—if you are still of the same mind, you shall hear the Massachusetts story."

CHAPTER XVI
WHAT MASSACHUSETTS CONTRIBUTED

M R. M CPHEARSON had no chance to forget his promise even had he been so minded, for promptly the next morning, almost before his tools were laid out on his bench, Christopher presented himself, announcing with a mischievous smile:

"To-day, you know, you are going to tell me the clock history of Massachusetts."

"Indeed I'm not," growled the Scotchman, who although flattered by the demand, was unwilling to admit it. "History of Massachusetts! The very idea!"

"I said the clock history," corrected Christopher, not a whit abashed.

"Did you? Well, even that is bad enough. What do you think I'm here for? To play school-master?"

"Oh, no, indeed. Merely to serve as my private tutor," was the teasing reply.

"That's your belief, is it! Egad, I begin to think it is," laughed the clockmaker, amused at the lad's audacity. "Certainly your demand would seem to bear out the theory."

"But you made the promise yourself—you can't have forgotten that."

"Forget it! Would I be likely to forget—would I so much as

get the chance, with you pestering me almost before my hat is off? Well, if I was rash enough to make a promise like that, I see no way but to keep it; so the Massachusetts clock story it shall be. It happens, too, that you have asked for it at just the right moment, for to-day I am going to work on as fine an old Willard clock as ever you saw. She is the real thing!"

"Was Willard the first of the Massachusetts clockmakers?"

"Among the first; and undeniably one of the best and most important of them. Oh, of course there were other men—some of them excellent. But we know less about them because they left no such long trail of clocks behind as the Willards did. Gawen Brown was a splendid workman; and so was Avery, who in 1726 made the clock for the Old North church. Then there was Benjamin Bagnall, who located in Charlestown about 1712 and remained there almost thirty years. His two sons, Benjamin and Samuel, also went into the clockmaking business and did very commendable work. In addition there were the Munroes of Concord—Daniel and Nathaniel; and Samuel Whiting, Nate's partner; not to mention the Popes, Robert and Joseph; and Daniel Balch of Newburyport. All these men were well established in or near Boston either before 1800 or shortly after that date."

"Evidently the Massachusetts people must have known what time it was," grinned Christopher.

"If they didn't it was their own fault," returned his companion, "for this list probably represents only a part of those engaged in the business. A good many more, like our friend, John Bailey, moved to small inland villages where they modestly plied their trade, selling their wares to only a limited circle of purchasers. Of these scattered craftsmen we have, as I told you, scant information. It is merely when we chance upon their names in early town records or a clock turns up to testify to their knowledge of their craft that we have tidings of them. But with the Willards it was different. They have left behind them a collection of clocks that speaks in no mistakable terms for their skill and industry."

"How many of these Willards were there?" Christopher demanded.

"Well, old Benjamin, the father, who was located in Framingham somewhere about the year 1716, had twelve children and three of these—Benjamin, Junior, Simon, and Aaron all became crackajack clockmakers, especially Simon. The family, I take it, went to Grafton, a small town near Worcester, later on. At any rate Benjamin, Junior, was born there. We afterward hear of him in Lexington and are told that in 1771 he moved from there to Roxbury. In this latter spot he himself set up a shop; but he must still have maintained another one at Grafton, his birthplace, where apprentices in the meantime carried on a part of his business, for his clocks bear three different markings—Grafton, Lexington, and Roxbury. He turned out excellent long-case clocks as well as some musical ones, and many of these survive him. He died in Baltimore in 1803. Aaron, and his son Aaron, Junior (who entered his father's shop in 1823), also made fine long-case clocks with brass works that found ready sale."

"And Simon?"

"Ah, the story of Simon and his deeds would fill a book. He was the flower of the family, so far, anyway, as clockmaking went. His handiwork cannot be surpassed," exclaimed McPhearson with enthusiasm. "People are liable to associate him only with the banjo clock that bears his name; but in reality he made clocks of every imaginable description—long-case clocks, tower clocks, gallery clocks, shelf clocks. He was a born clock lover if ever there was one! He was, moreover, a marvelous man who up to the end of his long life was active and useful.

Even after he became very old he fought to conceal the limitations age brought and remain cheerful and independent. A wonderful example of lusty manhood, truly! In the first place you must remember he started out on his career with the same meager equipment that hampered all the early clockmakers. A file, drill and hammer were practically the only tools he possessed. Neither you nor I would think it possible to construct so delicate a mechanism as a clock with so few articles to work with. We should insist that we needed and *must have* this thing, that thing, and the other thing to use, and then we probably should not be able to produce a clock that would go—let alone one that would keep accurate time. But you did not hear Simon Willard doing any fussing. There was nothing of the whiner about him. The fact that he was obliged to import brass from England, hammer it down to the thickness necessary, file it until it was smooth, and then polish it by hand did not daunt him. A more persistent, painstaking, conscientious clockmaker never lived. What marvel that he scorned to advertise? While others cried their products, he simply pasted in the back of each of his clocks the few modest facts he wished to announce and let his work go out to speak for itself."

"*Ask the man who owns one!*" put in Christopher, quoting a well-known and modern advertisement.

"Exactly!" agreed McPhearson. "Anybody that produces an A1 commodity hardly needs to bark about it. People find out what goods are worth. This, evidently, was Simon Willard's theory. You see he knew his trade from A to Z, having been apprenticed to his older brother Benjamin when only a small boy. The tale is that when barely thirteen years old he made a grandfather clock that was in every respect better than that of his master."

"Gee! Why, I am—"

"You are older than that already and could not make a clock, eh?" interrupted the Scotchman with quick understanding. "Neither could I, and I am many times your age. But life was different in the olden days. Boys learned trades very early and went to work at them. Many a lad, for example, was sent to sea by the time he was ten or twelve. Hence the fact that Simon Willard was apprenticed when so young was in no way remarkable. But that he should thus early have outranked his teacher is significant. We are not surprised, in consequence, to hear that it was not long before he branched out for himself and opened a shop at Grafton where he began to construct clocks."

"He must still have been pretty youthful," ventured Christopher.

"I imagine he was. Nevertheless he married and settled down to his career, starting in to make both shelf and long-case varieties. These he completed during the snowy season when the roads were bad and then, as soon as summer came and it was possible to get about on horseback, he and his brother, Aaron, used to travel about and sell the winter's output. Aaron peddled the goods along the south edge of the Massachusetts coast and Simon went north, sometimes even as far as Maine."

"But I should think clocks would have been ruined if jolted about on horseback!" objected Christopher.

"I don't think it could have been ideal for their health," laughed McPhearson. "But it was the best method of distribution the age afforded and Simon Willard did not scorn so humble a beginning. He remained in Grafton until some time between 1777 and 1780 and then as his wife died he moved to Roxbury and at what is now Number 2196 Washington Street opened a shop. In the meantime he had done quite a lot of experimenting and had arrived at the conclusion he would in future center his energy on making only church clocks, hall clocks and turret clocks. Therefore from that date on these were the styles he chiefly manufactured. Probably it would have been no small surprise to him had he known that the banjo clock he patented about 1802 and dubbed an *improved timepiece* would be the one to come down through history bearing his name."

"I wouldn't mind having it bear mine," smiled the boy, as he glanced toward the beautiful old Willard lying so ignominiously on its back on McPhearson's workbench. "I like all these brass trimmings. Besides, the picture of the sea fight painted on the glass door is jolly."

"Evidently Willard thought sea fights jolly, too, for he generally selected them as decoration for his clocks. I have heard there were two men in Roxbury who painted all his glass for him; one of them did lacy patterns of conventional design, and the other did naval battles. This fact helps us some in identifying genuine Willards. Of course the decoration could be copied by others; but add to it other hallmarks typical and now well-known and a true Willard can usually be detected. For instance, it is said on good authority that no real Willard clock is ever surmounted by a brass eagle. We often see the design on old clocks that purport to be Willards; but Simon Willard, his descendants attest, never used a decoration so elaborate. Instead he preferred simple things such as a brass acorn or one carved from wood; a gilt ball, or combination of ball and spear-head. But the eagle he never patronized."

"Maybe he didn't know how to make a brass eagle and couldn't find anybody who did," suggested Christopher.

"Possibly. To make an eagle would be quite an undertaking if you didn't know just how to set about it," acquiesced McPhearson. "At any rate Simon let eagles alone. Another device characteristic of his clocks, along with these two patterns of glass and the decoration on top, was the catch that kept the doors tightly closed. It was a pet scheme of his to make use of a sort of clasp that could only be opened with the clock key. This he resorted to in order to prevent the doors from jarring open and admitting the dirt; and also that children might not be able to meddle with the works or hands. He had a great many small children himself and had perhaps learned from experience the pranks little people were likely to perpetrate. Besides these several trademarks there are in addition various ingenious tricks that belonged to Willard and to nobody else. These a trained clockmaker instantly recognizes—the use of brass pins to hold the dial in place, for one thing. So, you see, when a banjo clock comes your way there are various methods by which its genuineness can be tested. They cannot, perhaps, be rated as infallible but they do help in identification."

"It is a pity Simon Willard did not sign his clocks as artists sign their pictures. Then there would have been no discussion about them," said Christopher.

"Willard did mark his later clocks," answered McPhearson. "Possibly in his early days it did not occur to him that it was worth while."

"Well, anyhow, I can hunt for the Willard tags—the queer catch on the door; the acorns, balls, or spearheads; and the painted lace or the naval battles."

At the final phrase the Scotchman smiled whimsically.

"It is funny Willard should have been so keen on sea fights," remarked he, "for as a matter of fact he was anything but a fighter. Undoubtedly it was the Revolution and the War of 1812 that stimulated the picturing of such scenes and made them popular. Had war been left to dear peace-loving old Simon Willard there would not have been much shooting, for he hated the very sight of a gun. One of his relatives declares that although like other loyal citizens he turned out at Lexington on the famous nineteenth of April and marched to Roxbury with Captain Kimball's company he often humorously asserted afterward that the musket he carried had no lock on it. The omission, however, did not appear to trouble him; on the contrary, it rather pleased him. Once, in later life, he one day picked up a gun that unexpectedly went off with such a bang that it knocked him down and as a result he could never be tempted into touching firearms of any description. The argument that they were not loaded had no effect whatsoever.

"No matter," he would say. "The durn thing may go off just the same."

Christopher laughed merrily.

"It was sometime between 1777 and 1780, as I told you, that Simon Willard came to Roxbury. But before he focused his entire attention on clocks he invented a clock-jack, and in 1784 with the approval of John Hancock, the General Court of Massachusetts granted him the exclusive right to make and sell the device."

"And what, pray, is a clock-jack?" interrogated Christopher.

"Ah, it is easily seen you did not live in early colonial days," smiled McPhearson. "A clock-jack, sonny, is a contrivance for roasting meat."

"Roasting meat!" repeated the lad incredulously. "But what had a man of Willard's genius to do with roasting meat?"

"Perhaps a good deal," the Scotchman answered. "He was the father of a big family, remember, and no doubt, like all good husbands, bore his share of the domestic burden. A man with eleven children must have been forced to turn his shoulder to the wheel in many a domestic crisis, for nobody kept servants at that time. Evidently either Willard himself had encountered the dilemmas of cooking or he had seen others struggle with them, and this, no doubt, was what led him to invent the ingenious article of which I have told you."

"But you haven't told me," was Christopher's quick protest.

"Why, so I haven't! Well, in the far-away days of our fore-fathers food was cooked neither in ranges nor in gas stoves. Instead it was cooked before the big open fire. A piece of meat, for example, was suspended by a chain from the mantelpiece and some member of the family was detailed to whirl it round and round until it was roasted evenly and cooked through. Now such an operation was a great nuisance, for no matter what you wished to do you must keep your mind on that roast lest it burn on one side and be ruined. If the mother of the house was washing dishes, cooking, or taking care of the baby, she had to stop every few moments and turn the meat around. And if she was too much occupied to do it, like as not the father was routed out of his shop, and told to have an eye on the beef.

"Willard himself may frequently have been forced to drop his tools and, since his children were young and motherless, attend to this bothersome duty. For fathers played a more intimate part in the homes of that generation than they do now. At any rate he was certainly familiar with the problems that entered into the cooking of the family dinner—just how heavy and clumsy were the big, awkward clock-jacks imported from England, how costly they were, and all. So he took the matter in hand and invented a clock-jack that was much better than the imported one. Not only did it spin the meat around when wound up, but it was enclosed in a brass cover that kept in the heat and juices. It is probable that the invention furnished inspiration for somebody else for presently the covered tin baker made its appearance and Willard abandoned making clock-jacks and turned his energy toward timekeepers instead."

"Do you mean to say he made his clocks at home?"

"At first he did. His house was a tiny dwelling, too. Just how he and his many children contrived to find places to sleep is a mystery. Some of the youngsters were tucked away in trundle beds, you may be sure. Out behind the kitchen was a sort of woodshed, and it was in this primitive location that Mr. Willard made his clocks."

"Not big clocks!"

"Yes, indeed."

"But I should think he would have been compelled to have more room."

"I fancy his quarters were not ideal and were pretty cramped. He could have got on well enough had he been making shelf clocks that vibrated only half-seconds, like those of Eli Terry; but he had given up making those when he left Grafton. Therefore when it came to testing out his big turret clocks, he had to cut a hole in the floor in order to give their long pendulums room to swing."

"That was a stunt!"

"It simply proves that a determined man will find a way," McPhearson declared. "Simon Willard was not a person who allowed circumstances to master him. Lack of tools, limitations of space, the utter absence of all those aids we should now deem indispensable—none of these obstacles deterred him from making clocks that have seldom been outranked."

"A bully good sport, wasn't he!" exclaimed Christopher.

"A sport in the best sense," agreed McPhearson. "As a humble member of his craft I take off my hat to him. It was in 1801 that he made his first banjo clock—a clock that, as he asserted, could be hung on the wall and stood no risk of being knocked off or moved about as a shelf clock did. The patent for this article bore the autographs of President Jefferson and James Madison, who was at the time Secretary of State. The same year Willard made a clock for the United States Senate Chamber and went to Washington to assure himself that it was properly put up and also explain how it should be cared for. This clock, unfortunately, was ruined when the British burned the Capitol; nevertheless, Willard's journey hither was not in vain, for while in the city he made the personal acquaintance of President Jefferson and the two men, both of them interested in mechanics, formed a lifelong friendship. In fact, it was through Jefferson that Willard received the order to make a large clock for the University of Virginia."

"And did he have to go down there, too?"

"He did go down. During Jefferson's lifetime he was more than once a guest at Monticello. The clock, however, was not completed until after the President died, and when Willard finally went to put it in place he stayed with Madison who had a home no great distance away."

"He seemed to make friends wherever his business took him," remarked Christopher thoughtfully.

"Not only that, but his work made friends for him," was McPhearson's answer. "It was so well done that people appreciated its worth and gave him more orders. For fifty years he had charge of the clocks at Harvard University and in 1829 the Corporation awarded him a vote of thanks for his faithful services. It is something of a record to have performed work so satisfactorily for half a century."

"I'll say it is!"

"In 1837 the United States Government engaged Mr. Willard to make two clocks for the new Capitol at Washington, one of them to take the place of the Senate clock that was burned and the other to be put in Statuary Hall. In the latter room there was already a very beautiful allegorical clock but it needed new works. Willard was now getting to be an old man and such a commission would have dismayed most elderly persons. But although eighty-five the old clockmaker did not hesitate to fill the order or travel to Washington to make sure his handiwork was properly installed. It sometimes seemed as if he must have discovered the fountain of eternal youth. Remember he was seventy-eight when he made the turret clock for the Old State House in Boston. I have heard that for some of this later work he used a hand engine to cut parts afterward finished by hand; and of course as his fame traveled and his business increased, he had apprentices to help him and he was obliged to move into a larger shop. But even at that the miracle of what he did does not lose its luster.

"At length, in 1839, he retired, a hale, respected veteran with a long path of usefulness behind him. Until he was eighty he read without glasses; and so accurate was his eye that never in all his life did he measure the notchings on a wheel, and yet these free-hand calculations proved to be unfailingly correct. But, alas, human machinery is less long-lived than is artificial, and at the age of ninety-five Simon Willard died.

"*'The old clock is worn out!* was what he said, and indeed the words were true. For close on to a century eyes, hands, and brain had continuously labored for the well-being of others. Yet the works of a good man follow him and in numberless homes, in public buildings, on church spires, honored monuments to the memory of Simon Willard still survive—monuments far more useful than are inert blocks of marble—monuments that pulse with life and keep hourly before those who look upon them the thought of one who performed for his fellow men a practical and enduring service."

CHAPTER XVII
THE ROMANCE OF THE WATCH

"I ASKED Dad last night why he didn't have a Willard clock here in the store instead of the one we've got," confided Christopher to McPhearson the next morning, "and he was quite sore about it. He said that in the first place a balcony clock of Willard make would cost a fortune and probably could not be bought, anyway; and then he added that we already had a Jim-dandy clock made by one of the Willard apprentices. I didn't get the chance to ask him what he meant by that."

"Our clock is a Howard, one of the best makes there is," McPhearson explained. "Years ago Edward Howard, the founder of the Howard Clock Company, began clockmaking as a pupil of Aaron Willard, Junior. Howard was a boy of only sixteen at the time, and for five years he studied clocks under this excellent tutelage. Do not imagine, however, that this balcony clock of ours was made by Mr. Howard himself. What your father meant was that built into the background of the Howard Company were the Willard traditions and ideas."

"Then really Aaron Willard hadn't much to do with our clock," remarked Christopher, disappointment in his voice.

"Not directly, no. Still you have no cause for complaint on that score. The Howard clock is a more modern product, that is all. Mr. Howard, like Mr. Willard, left his imprint on both the American clock and watch industries, holding for years a very unique place in their development. Moreover he founded a great business that now gives to us clocks of almost every design. Many are for the interiors of public buildings such as halls, stores, churches, offices, and railway stations. Others are for towers or steeples. Some have illuminated dials and some are electric watch clocks. Therefore do not waste your tears lamenting that your father does not possess an old Willard balcony clock. It would be an interesting thing to own, I don't deny that; but what you already have is as good a timepiece as can be procured anywhere. No one blushes for a Howard clock or needs to blush. Mr. Howard, along with Willard, deserves great credit for building up this successful business of his, for when he began it he started out all by himself in a little shop not over thirty feet square."

"It's a wonderful thing to found a big business, isn't it?" reflected Christopher.

"Yes, to set going a flourishing industry that not only provides bread and butter for hundreds of workmen but also furnishes the public with a well-made commodity that it needs is a great service to civilization," said McPhearson. "Edward Howard, as I told you, had a generous part in doing this, not only in the clock world but also in the realm of watches."

"How did he connect up with the watches?"

"Well, you see, early America had very few watchmakers," was the reply. "There were, it is true, numerous persons who dubbed themselves watchmakers and who, like myself, could repair a watch; but they could not make one. Therefore watch-making as an industry did not exist in this country. So about 1850 Mr. Aaron Dennison, a Boston watch repairer, conceived the idea of starting such a business. Already he had discussed plans with Edward Howard, and now the two men entered into partnership and after raising considerable capital they constructed a small factory in Roxbury. To fully appreciate the difficulties of their venture, you must keep in mind the fact that previous to this time watchmaking had never been conducted along modern lines. There was no such thing in the world as a factory system where every part of a watch was made beneath one roof. Instead, as I believe I told you, watches were made in different places—the wheels at the home of one man, the springs at that of another, and so on, after which the various parts were assembled, put together, and adjusted. This was the plan followed in France, England, and Switzerland, and the one which with certain modifications is to a great extent still followed in those countries. And in our own land there was not even as much of a system as that, watches being made on a very small scale by individual workmen. It was this scheme of affairs that Aaron Dennison and Edward Howard determined to change."

"They took some contract on their hands, I should say."

"A bigger contract than you realize, son," the Scotchman answered. "A bigger one than they fully realized, I guess. It is fortunate we do not see all our obstacles when we set forth on an undertaking, for if we did many an enterprise would be abandoned before it was even begun. These two men, now— in the first place they had no machinery; nor was there any to be bought. Moreover, there was nothing to pattern watch machinery after. It had never been made. So, you see, it was one thing to give a man tools and leave him to achieve with them a specified end, working toward the desired result as he went along; and quite another to invent a brainless device that would mechanically reach the same end. Numberless difficulties must be overcome. To manufacture watches in quantity it was imperative that the parts be interchangeable. They must not vary even an infinitesimal degree or the whole delicate organism would be thrown out of adjustment. It was not an industry where hit-or-miss methods could be glossed over; on the contrary, every part of the process must be absolutely accurate. Do you wonder people were skeptical as to the possibility of making such a mad undertaking a success and hesitated about putting money into it?"

"I suppose the public rated it a wildcat scheme," responded Christopher.

"Yes, it seemed very impractical to business men. When you have to build up a factory system from the machinery itself, you have something gigantic on your hands. And that is the task on which Mr. Dennison and Mr. Howard embarked. I suppose nobody will ever appreciate the trials those dauntless pioneers went through. Four years they worked in their Roxbury factory and only had a few hundred watches to show for all their toil. Nevertheless the experience taught them many things and chief among these was the fact that they must have more room. Accordingly in 1854 they put up a new factory at Waltham, Massachusetts, and it is this structure, standing to this day, that was the first building of the Waltham Watch factory."

"So the Waltham Watch factory is the grandfather of all the others, is it?" commented Christopher.

"It is both the oldest and the largest," declared McPhearson. "It also is the place where the factory system of watch manufacture had its beginning. The general disbelief of the public was, however, a great obstacle to the prosperity of the infant enterprise. Often both Mr. Dennison and Mr. Howard were bitterly disheartened. The outlay for constructing machinery, buying materials, and experimenting licked up capital with terrifying rapidity. Had not two Boston men, Mr. Samuel Curtis and Mr. Charles Rice, had faith enough to back the project financially, it certainly would have gone to pieces. Even as it was quantities of money were sunk before any results were forthcoming. The parts of a watch are so small and so delicate that to produce machinery that would make them and make them so that one did not vary from another by so much as a hair-breadth—well, there were moments when it seemed almost futile to try to do it. For, you know, if any part of a watch is even so much as one five-thousandth of an inch out of the way, it is good-by to the watch. It won't go—that is all!"

"I had no idea such a variation as that would count for anything," gasped his listener. "Why, it must have been terrible to figure machinery down to that point! I shouldn't think Mr. Dennison or Mr. Howard would ever have wanted to look at another watch."

"I imagine there were times when they didn't," was McPhearson's grave response. "But for all that they persisted. Fortunately they made a pretty good team, so far as training went, for Mr. Dennison was perfectly familiar with repairing, and Mr. Howard with the construction of watches. Notwithstanding this, however, neither of them had any knowledge whatsoever as to certain details of the business—how to make a dial, temper hairsprings, polish steel, or do watch-gilding properly—and none of their men had either. As a result every one of these separate arts and many like them had to be studied and mastered from the foundation up, and after the chiefs themselves had experimented and found out how to turn the trick they had to teach their men what they personally had learned."

"Great Scott! I'd have given the business away to anybody who wanted it," burst out Christopher.

"So would almost anybody else, I fancy," agreed the Scotchman. "But they kept right on sticking at it. It wasn't their courage that gave out in the end; it was their money. They simply could not continue to pull along under so colossal a burden. Therefore after three years they sold the business (operated at that time under the name of the Boston Watch Company) to Mr. Royal Robbins, and he reorganized it and christened it the Waltham Watch Company."

"It seems kind of a pity they had to sell it," mused Christopher with regret. "The worst of the battle was over by that time."

"Yes. At least the foundation of the enterprise was well laid."

"What became of Mr. Dennison and Mr. Howard?" asked the boy.

"Mr. Howard went back to Roxbury to his first factory and there the Howard Watch and Clock Company was formed. The saying goes that it is a long lane that has no turning. Certainly every one familiar with Mr. Howard's early struggles must have rejoiced in the success that ultimately came to him. Mr. Dennison had in the meantime left the Waltham company; but when it was reorganized he returned to it and remained there several years to lend his invaluable aid to the new firm."

"And did the concern go ahead after that?"

"Yes, it had reached calm waters by this time. Besides, when the Civil War arose and the rate of gold went up, watches brought very high prices and the company coined money. With it they were enabled to branch out and not only improve their home plant but put up factories elsewhere. Some of these were not, to be sure, successful; but as a whole the business thrived wonderfully. Offices were established in London, and America began to take her place among the big watchmaking countries of the world."

"Hurrah for Uncle Sam!" laughed the boy.

"Rather I say hurrah for the fellows who fought his watch battle for him," was McPhearson's somewhat curt retort. "For the watch business has never been one easy of development. You can blunder along and turn out poor, carelessly made stuff in certain lines of trade and get by with it. The public does not always know a good product from a bad one, and all except the expert can be easily fooled. But a watch proclaims its own worth. It has to go and has to keep accurate time or all the world will know it. If it fails to do the work it was bought to do, people won't buy it. Therefore that these results may be reached and a satisfactory article put on the market there must be money enough to house a large plant, pay skilled and high-priced workmen, supply the best of material, and tempt into the industry men of brains. Many a watch venture has gone on the rocks for the lack of these assets.

"Once on its feet, however, a well-manned American watch concern has all it can do. It need have no qualms about foreign rivalry, for no European country has ever yet been able to build up a factory system that could touch that of the United States, either in quality or quantity of output. As a result most nations have given over trying to. Our watches can be made cheaper and hence in greater numbers than those of other lands, and we now practically control the watch market. The era when a few watches were made by hand and afterward sent to a local astronomer or distant observatory to be tested out has passed. Even before the United States Naval Observatory was established the Waltham Watch Company had an observatory of its own. Now we have graduated even beyond that point and each noon the official time is telegraphed or broadcast from Arlington to all parts of the country."

"We do whizz ahead, don't we?" meditated Christopher, absently twirling between his fingers a screw he had picked up from McPhearson's bench.

"I should say we did," was the enthusiastic reply. "That screw, for instance! In the infancy of watchmaking it took a good factory worker a whole day to make from eight to twelve hundred screws. This seems a vast number until you recall that each watch requires from thirty to fifty of these small articles. At that rate, you see, it would not take long to use up all the screws a mechanic could turn out. Now, so marvelous has machinery become, that a single operator can tend half a dozen or more machines, every one of which can produce from four thousand to ten thousand screws a day. This gives you some idea of the proportionate increase in watch parts. For in a big country like this we have to make lots of watches to supply those constantly clamoring for them. Long ago a watch was either a toy or a luxury; but now every person you meet carries one. The price is such that he can afford to. But more than this, a watch is absolutely indispensable in our present manner of living. From morning to night we rush to crowd into our twenty-four hours everything we can possibly crowd in; and in order to do this we must keep careful track of the minutes and hours. Hence the demand for watches has multiplied almost beyond belief and there are now a great many watch factories."

"What are some of them?"

"I'll mention a few as nearly in the order of their founding as I can," McPhearson answered:

"The E. Howard Company of Boston, organized 1850.

"American Waltham Watch Company, Waltham, Massachusetts, 1859.

"Elgin National Watch Company, Elgin, Illinois, 1870.

"Rockford Watch Company, Rockford, Illinois, 1874.

"U. S. Watch Company, Waltham, Massachusetts, 1883.

"Hamilton Watch Company, Lancaster, Pennsylvania, 1892.

"These are some of the oldest and best known firms."

Christopher thought a moment.

"Of course I've heard of some of them," remarked he. "The Hamilton everybody knows. It is advertised in almost every magazine."

"The Hamilton watch came into being under interesting and, I may say, tragic circumstances. One day a bad railroad accident happened out near Cleveland, Ohio, and when the calamity was investigated evidence proved that neither of the engineers on the unlucky trains that collided was really to blame. The trouble was that their watches did not agree. There was a difference of four minutes between them. Both timepieces were good ones that never before had led their owners astray; but on this fatal day they were responsible not only for the deaths of two blameless engineers but also a number of mail clerks. It is strange, isn't it, that the public must always experience a terrible lesson before it wakes up to safeguarding human life? Let us have a fire in which many persons perish, and we begin to move heaven and earth to inspect buildings and install fire escapes; or let a lot of people die from shipwreck and we cannot buy life belts fast enough. But we always wait until *after* the disaster has occurred before we do it. Thus it was with this fatal railroad accident. Once the catastrophe had happened and the poor chaps were dead, a set of rules was established whereby men employed on trains must carry watches of a specified quality. No cheap article was to be allowed in future. And not only must the railroad worker purchase such a watch, but he must keep it cleaned and properly regulated."

"That was all very well to decree," replied Christopher, "but how could the authorities make sure such a rule would be obeyed?"

"Ah, the railroad took no chances of being fooled," was McPhearson's instant reply. "A watch inspector was appointed whose duty it was to examine every important official's watch once in a stated period and see that it conformed to the requirements. If a watch failed to keep up to the standard set—by that I mean if it lost or gained more than a very trifling amount a week—it was condemned and ordered to be discarded and a new one had to be bought."

"But how about the men?" put in Christopher, a hint of disapproval in his tone. "What if some of them couldn't afford to purchase these fine-running, expensive watches? Being told to toss your watch out the window and get another isn't always possible."

"It was to meet the objection that you have just raised that a week after the wreck the Hamilton Watch Company of Lancaster was organized. It aimed to manufacture a good, close-running watch at a moderate price, and it fulfilled its promise. The proposition was a sound business one, too, for all over the country men were employed to whom correctness of time was of vital importance—switch-tenders, motormen, engineers, conductors, not to enumerate the thousands of other working people to whom being prompt at ferries, trains, cars, and their job was imperative. So, you see, the age provided a distinct market for a high-class article of this sort and the Hamilton Company was intelligent enough to realize and seize it. Good business is seeing your chance, grabbing it, and then holding onto it."

The lad smiled.

"Of course there are times," continued McPhearson, "when it is possible to create a market out of whole cloth. If, for instance, you can think of something that would be useful to the public, something they themselves have never happened to think of before, you can bring it to their attention by clever advertising and make them want it. That is the method the Waterbury Watch Company followed in launching their goods back in 1880. For a long time two Massachusetts men had been wondering whether an exceedingly cheap watch that would be within the reach of even quite poor people could not be made. Such a commodity, they argued, could not fail to have an extensive sale. The problem was who could they find to construct this sort of timepiece? Then on a fine day Mr. Locke, one of the men, saw in the window of a Worcester jeweler a miniature steam engine that had previously been exhibited at the Philadelphia Centennial. Immediately the thought came into his mind that a workman who could construct such a perfect toy must be both ingenious and inventive, and he went into the shop and offered Mr. Buck, the maker of the wee engine, a hundred dollars to produce for him a cheap watch of the type he had in mind."

"Was Mr. Buck ready to try the stunt?"

"Yes, he agreed to see what he could do," was the reply. "So he got to work and after a little while had a model ready. But, alas, it did not prove to be much of a watch, and the poor man, having toiled and worried about it day and night, finally went to bed sick. But of course that wouldn't do. He had had the money and therefore was bound either to pay it back—a thing he was in too straitened circumstances to do—or he must stick at the problem until he solved it. Both he and his wife were honest people who understood this. Accordingly Mrs. Buck begged that her husband be given a little more time. He had, declared she, a better plan in his head which he would try out as soon as he was able."

"What did Mr. Locke say to that?"

"Both he and Mr. Merritt, his associate, consented to wait a little while and at the end of a few months Mr. Buck was as good as his word and brought them the model of a watch that was exactly what they wanted. Thus far the enterprise went all right." The clockmaker paused.

"You sound as if things began to happen afterward," suggested Christopher.

"Well, to tell the truth, they did. In the first place money had to be raised to put the venture on its feet. As a good deal of this capital, together with factory facilities, was offered by a brass manufacturing firm at Waterbury, Connecticut, there the plant was installed. But like every other watchmaking project this one swallowed up a great many dollars before any watches were to be seen. Then at last the first thousand were triumphantly turned out and, to the chagrin of the firm, proved to be anything but a success. Some difficulty with the brass used prevented their running properly."

One would have thought, to hear Christopher's sympathetic exclamation, that all his earnings had been invested in the unlucky enterprise.

"The second thousand were better," went on the Scotchman, "but still they did not go well; this meant more money to improve the machinery and still more delay in putting the goods on the market. Then at length after the watches had been doctored until only a small percentage of them stopped they were offered for sale."

"Did people buy them?"

"If they didn't it was not the fault of the Company," chuckled McPhearson. "Certainly every inducement was held out to purchasers. Not only was the price of four dollars within reach of the most meager purse, but the watches were dangled as bait before the eyes of all sorts of covetous bargain hunters. Sometimes you were coaxed into buying a suit of clothes to get one; sometimes one came with a big order of groceries or maybe as a premium for selling soap. Not infrequently they were awarded as prizes for subscriptions to magazines. They were so hawked about that the whole country heard of them and quantities of them were sold."

"The firm must have got rich," put in Christopher, much interested.

"It didn't," was the prompt contradiction. "On the contrary, after several years of struggle, it failed. The public is fickle, you know, and the novelty of owning a cheap watch wore off. Moreover, the product got a bad name and failed to be taken seriously. It required a great deal of time and energy to wind a watch with such a long spring as this one had, and I must agree that those who made jokes at the expense of the poor Waterbury were well within their rights. Furthermore, the watches had been linked up with inferior commodities and when purchasers found, for example, that they had been gulled on the suit of clothes they acquired with the watch, instead of cursing the clothier they took out their wrath on the watch company. Then, too, the firm, in order to get their wares distributed, had parted with them at so small a margin of profit that nothing was made on them. The entire scheme from beginning to end showed poor generalship. What wonder such an enterprise went down?"

"And is that the end of the story?"

"By no means," retorted the Scotchman. "Far from it. The management took their experience as wise people do and years later began over again, afterward reaping greater success than they had ever known, all of which proves that it never pays to give up."

"Haven't lots of other kinds of cheap watches been made since?"

"Yes. The Ingersoll is one. It is the result of several years' experiment with a dollar watch. At first a thick, clumsy contrivance that wound from the back like a clock was introduced, and from this stepping stone Ingersoll developed a second and third type, each an improvement on the original. Having thereby convinced himself that the dollar watch was not only possible but would sell, he got the Waterbury Company to put out his idea for him; now the Ingersolls have in addition two factories of their own, and the three together average an output of about twenty thousand watches a day. In a country as big as ours, however, the great problem is to get goods known from east to west, and from the north to the south, and this obstacle of distribution was the one the company encountered. How was the country generally to know there was a good dollar watch? Owing to the scant margin of profit on which the watches were sold, it did not pay large retailers to carry them. Neither could they find even standing-room in a shop like your fathers'." With dancing eyes the Scotchman regarded Christopher.

"Moreover," he went on, "although Ingersoll guaranteed his watch, tricky competition arose. Other firms borrowed the name as a label for their own poor goods; some merchants took the Ingersoll watch and ran up the price on it, privately pocketing the profit. To outwit such practices the company not only printed their name on the dials of their watches but they carefully printed the exact price on the boxes in which they were packed. You would have thought this would have forever put at an end any foul play, wouldn't you? But even these precautions were circumvented by sharpers who advertised their wretched wares as marked-down Ingersolls. Thus the company was compelled to fight inch by inch for its rights."

"I'd no idea business was such a mess," ejaculated Christopher. "And what happened to the Ingersoll people finally?"

"Providentially a turn came in their affairs," was the answer. "It is an ill wind that blows nobody good, the saying goes. In every calamity lurks some good and for the Ingersoll Company, at least, there was good in the Great War. Again we see a clever manufacturer grasping his opportunity. No one knew better than Ingersoll how costly striking watches were; he also sensed that soldiers who were fighting could not be supplied with endless numbers of watches nor even if they were would they always be where they could show a light. Nevertheless there would be hundreds of men in the trenches and on the battle fields who through long stretches of darkness would wish to know what time it was. Many would be on guard and compelled to remain awake; and many more would be unable to sleep from terror, homesickness, or because they suffered from the various discomforts war brings. What, therefore, could be a greater boon than a cheap watch with an illuminated face? It was to answer this emergency that the Ingersoll Company turned out their Radiolite Watch."

"I suppose the dial had phosphorus on it," rejoined Christopher.

"No. Phosphorus was found to be entirely impractical for the purpose, because, you see, phosphorus must at intervals be placed where it can absorb the light in order to retain its brilliancy. Now as a man's watch stays most of the time in his pocket, a watch dial treated with phosphorus would have no opportunity to regain its phosphorescence. Hence the Ingersoll Company developed a sort of radium coating for their dials. It probably was not actually made from radium because there is not enough of it to be found in all the world even if a watch company could afford to buy it up. Just what this magic watch dial was made from was Ingersoll's secret; but anyway it did what it was guaranteed to do and instantly leaped into popularity. Many and many a soldier off on the battle front blessed the makers of these watches, I guess. As for the company—no longer were they obliged to wrestle with the problem of getting their goods known, because from one end of our country to the other, as well as far overseas, their watches became a byword." The old Scotchman stopped as if tired with telling his long story.

"Now," added he, "I have roughly sketched for you the tale of watchmaking in America. There is much more that might be related but you yourself, by using your eyes and ears, can fill in the gaps. Just remember this one fact—that it was your own land that developed and brought to its present high grade of efficiency the factory system of making watches. You have no cause to apologize, either, for your country's handiwork. We do not by any means always hold first place in the products we put out. Many nations can give us points along certain lines of industry. But in this field we are supreme and have given the world something for which we need not blush. So, say I, three cheers for Uncle Sam! Sometime if you can manage it, make a trip through one of our up-to-date American watch factories. Examine the numberless machines that represent so much patient and intelligent study. Then come home grateful to our watch pioneers for what they have handed on to us."

CHAPTER XVIII
CHRISTOPHER HAS A BIRTHDAY

WHILE clocks and watches ticked on and rings and gemmed necklaces were sold to covetous buyers, the year was sweeping by and May was coming. Christopher always looked forward to this month, gay with flowers, for with it came his birthday—a date always celebrated with rejoicing in the Burton family.

It was the one time of year when he became of supreme importance and when everybody in the house united to turn the world upside down for his delight. Christmas was a general holiday. But May twentieth was his own particular anniversary. Always there was some really worthwhile present about which endless whispering and the greatest secrecy was maintained. Once it had been a fine camera; once a tool chest; last year it was the long-coveted wireless for which he had so long sighed. What, speculated the boy, would it be this season?

Thus far he had not gleaned an inkling. There had been times when in spite of his father's and mother's precautions to surprise him he had had suspicions; and occasionally such suspicions had proved to be right. His radio set, for example— he had been pretty sure it was coming, and on May twentieth there it was! And then there had been instances when measure- ments had to be taken or the size of his shoes considered, and these inevitable hints had given away beforehand the plots his parents were hatching.

But this year dense mystery hung like a curtain over the great day. There was not even a mention made of it. No casual remarks were dropped to trap him into telling what he wanted. Indeed, so dumb was every one concerning the festival that he actually began to fear the date had been forgotten. Of course a great deal of money had already been spent on his eyes; he realized that. He had been to the oculist almost every week for treatment. He knew he should be grateful for all this and he was. But despite what it had cost, one could hardly consider it a present. Still, as the days went by and there appeared to be no prospect of anything else in the wind, he began to believe his parents regarded it as one. Grown-ups looked at things from such a different angle! No doubt they felt they had spent upon him all they felt justified in spending.

This realization at first brought to the lad a sense of disappointment. There were so many things he wanted! Why, although he would have blushed to admit it, there was lying in his pocket this very minute a list of gifts carefully written out in case his father or mother asked for suggestions as they often had done in the past. But they did not inquire for it. May eighteenth and May nineteenth slipped by without an allusion to the fact that on May twentieth he had been born, and so oblivious was everybody to his existence that had he not looked in the glass and verified it, he would almost have begun to doubt he was alive himself.

When at length the great day dawned, he descended to breakfast with that mingled anticipation and self-consciousness that always overwhelmed him on such occasions. He was wont to feel very foolish and vividly aware of his hands and feet when he made his annual advent into the dining room.

As it happened, however, he need have experienced no embarrassment to-day for the fact that fourteen years ago he had entered into this vale of tears was not mentioned. True, his mother did kiss him a trifle more warmly than usual, and an additional salutation, which she instantly repressed, seemed trembling on her tongue. But there was nothing else out of the ordinary.

Therefore he sat down and ate his breakfast with the chagrined conviction that for the first time in history the anniversary to which he had habitually looked forward with such keen pleasure had slipped his parents' memory. It was strange that each of them should have forgotten. Even if his father had been too busy about the shipment of the gems expected from Holland to bear it in mind, one would have thought his mother would have remembered. She was, to be sure, much taken up with doing over the library and fussing about curtains which she declared she never would be able to match. But for all that you would have thought she would recall that May twentieth was coming. It wasn't at all like her to let her own interests crowd out those of her family.

Perhaps they thought he was getting too old for birthdays. That would be a tragedy indeed, since it would mean that he never would have any more presents. Oh, it wasn't likely they thought that! No, the whole thing was just a mistake, and as long as it was Christopher shrank from correcting the error. You couldn't very well shout, "This is my birthday, good people. Any contributions you would like to give me will be gratefully received." Once he would not have hesitated to do this. But now he was older and had more pride.

Therefore he ate his orange and his cereal as serenely as he could, hoping the disappointment he experienced would not be evident in his face. Apparently it was not. With customary impatience Mr. Burton swallowed his coffee and, rising from the table, cautioned his son to hurry up and not keep him waiting; and on hearing this familiar admonition, Christopher's last weak hope that the day was to be different from other days vanished, and he dashed for his hat and coat.

"Good-by, Mother," he called up the stairway.

"Your mother is going into town with us to-day," Mr. Burton explained. "She has some errands to do."

"She didn't say so at breakfast."

"She forgot to, most likely. She was in a good deal of a hurry. Here she comes now. Don't stop to put on your gloves, my dear. You can do it in the car."

Off they went to the station and then into New York they whizzed by train. There was not much opportunity to talk. Christopher's father read the paper, and his mother consumed the time by holding various scraps of gauzy blue stuff up to the light and asking which of them he liked best. Then they bundled into a taxi and riding to the store entered it, where the counterpart of every other day in the year began. And yet, after all, did the day start as other days were wont to do? To begin with, there was his mother who, instead of rolling off downtown to her shopping, as would have been her customary program, alighted from the taxicab with his father and himself. Moreover the interior of the shop did not seem quite the same. Nonsensical as it was to suppose it, there seemed to be in the atmosphere a subtle air of suspense quite new and unusual. Besides that, there were flowers on his father's desk; and what was more surprising, apparently he was the only one to notice these innovations.

Nevertheless he did not speak of them but pulled off his

coat and stood for a moment hesitating before going to hunt up McPhearson. It was in his mind to accompany his mother down in the elevator and see her to the door after she should have finished her business. Perhaps she had come to get money for her shopping; or possibly, as she sometimes did, she was going to select a wedding present downstairs. But if any such missions stimulated her she was, to judge by appearances, in no haste to fulfill them; instead she loosened her scarf and sat down as if she had no other aim in the world than to remain all day.

He couldn't quite make it out.

Then presently the door opened and in came Mr. Rhinehart, Hollings, McPhearson, and even the old colored elevator man, who every day had carried him up and down. Mr. Norcross also stole in from his office and so did the prim Miss Elkins.

Then, to the boy's astonishment, Mr. Rhinehart stepped forward and began a little speech. At first Christopher did not grasp the fact that it was directed to himself; but soon, when in the name of all the employees of his father's firm, the kindly clerk wished him a happy birthday and handed him a small red leather case, it gradually dawned on him that he was actually the hero of a surprise party.

The flowers, the tensity that pervaded the shop, his mother's coming to the city were all because on May twentieth, fourteen years ago, he had been born. The day had not been forgotten as he had thought. On the contrary, more people had this time thought of him and taken pains to let him know it than he had ever supposed cared whether he was alive or not. And to prove it, they were now giving him a present. Mr. Rhinehart, Hollings, McPhearson, old Saunders—all of them had had a part in it—and they said it was because they had become fond of him and admired him for being so cheerful and patient about his eyes. Their kindness overwhelmed him and brought a queer, tight, choky feeling into his throat. He didn't deserve any of the things Mr. Rhinehart said. It didn't seem to him that he had been very patient. On the contrary, he had often rebelled inside at being so helpless. How ashamed he was when he thought of his secret grumblings!

With pounding heart and cheeks that burned he looked down at the red leather case in his hand.

Think of the men doing this for him! He wanted to tell them how wonderful he thought it was, to tell them he didn't merit such a gift; but no words would come.

Then he heard his father speaking:

"I am sure, Christopher, you wish to thank Mr. Rhinehart and through him the others who have so generously given you this beautiful present."

"I do want to, Dad," cried he, looking up, "but you see I don't know how. I never was so surprised in all my life. It's knocked the breath out of me."

Laughter greeted this naïve confession. Then everything became easier.

"Suppose," suggested his mother, "you open the box and see what's in it."

The idea was a happy one. With action his shyness vanished and centering his attention on the square case in his hand a cry of pleasure escaped him. Lying there on the dark crimson velvet was a watch—a gold repeater—bearing the stamp of America's first and oldest watchmaking factory. He knew all about that particular watch, for he had often seen it in the show case and coveted it. And now, miracle of miracles, there it was in his hand with his own monogram adorning its back cover. He had never expected to possess anything so precious.

"You see, Christopher, we've all enjoyed having you round the store this winter," murmured McPhearson. "You've brought cheer to everybody. We shall miss you when you go back to school next season. Nevertheless we rejoice your eyes are on the mend and we wanted you to know how glad we are."

"It was bully of you all—simply bully!" burst out the lad. "I don't deserve anything of the sort, for I know I must have been more bother to everybody than I was worth. You are the ones who have been patient. But the watch is a dandy. It is exactly the one I would have picked out could I have had my choice. You see, I've never owned a line watch. I guess it was just as well, too, for I never appreciated watchmaking until Mr. McPhearson told me what a really good watch meant. Now I'd as soon starve a kitten as not take care of it."

A clapping of hands greeted the assertion.

"But you were wrong about one thing, Dad," the boy continued. "I am not going to thank the men through Mr. Rhinehart or anybody else. I am going round the store to thank every person myself."

"Bravo, son!" replied Mr. Burton. "But before you start on this pilgrimage I have just a word to add. The gift you hold in your hand has been presented to you by the men of Burton and Norcross. Your mother and I have had no part in it, and the present we have planned for you has not yet been delivered. It is a different sort from the one you usually receive from us. Nevertheless, although it is neither a wireless, a typewriter, a dog, or a bicycle I hope you are going to like it."

He paused for a moment and glanced round the office.

"There is one man in our employ who has been here longer than any of the others," he went on. "He is a man whom we all respect and whose loyalty and friendship we value highly.

Years ago he left his native land to become a citizen of this country and give to America his skill and knowledge. His faithful, intelligent labor has had much to do with the building up of our business and the establishment of a standard for thorough, reliable work. You all know the man I have in mind—Angus McPhearson."

Cheers broke in on the speech. The old Scotchman was a general favorite. It was easy to see that.

"This winter," added Mr. Burton, "this craftsman has annexed to his other duties that of tutor. He has taken you, Christopher, and taught you more in a few short months than I ever knew you to learn before in all your history. Because your mother and I are grateful to him for his kindness, interest, and instruction; because, as the head of this firm I value his services and wish to recognize them, I have selected for you a birthday present that shall include him. I know you like him very much—"

"You bet I do!" interrupted Christopher enthusiastically.

"And so," continued Mr. Burton, bestowing on the comment only a smile, "we have planned to send you two to Europe this summer on a clock-seeing expedition."

"Oh!" cried Christopher.

"Oh, sir!" came in a bewildered whisper from the Scotchman.

"You will first go to Scotland," explained Mr. Burton, "and there McPhearson is to visit his old home and the friends he wishes to hunt up. He is not to hurry about it, either. Then, while you are there, he is to take you for a trip through the Scotch Lakes that you may see the beauty of the land that turns out such splendid men as he. After that you will travel down through England, seeing all you can as you go and searching out the old clocks and the famous collections of them that he has told you about. Then across the Channel in an airship (you will like that, Christopher) and on to France, Switzerland, Germany, and Italy. How does the proposition strike you, son?"

"We'll see the bears of Berne, Mr. McPhearson," cried Christopher excitedly. "And the Straasburg clock, too! And that wonderful clock in Venice. Think of it!"

"I am scarcely able to think of it," gasped the little Scotchman.

"You would like to go?" inquired Mr. Burton gently.

"Oh, sir, it has been my dream for years. I have thought and thought of sometime making such a journey. But it never has been possible. The expense—"

"It is going to be possible now," cut in Mr. Burton, smiling. "That is, if you are willing to take Christopher along."

"Nothing would please me better," ejaculated the watchmaker. "He is a fine lad. This year I have come to—"

"We know you have, Mr. McPhearson," asserted Mrs. Burton softly. "Your kindness to our boy has proved that. That is why we are going to trust him to you. He is the most precious thing we have in the world. We should not let everybody borrow him."

With that the group broke up. Mr. Norcross hurried into his office; Mrs. Burton opened her bag and once more began to fumble with her foolish gauzy samples; and Mr. Burton took up from his desk a handful of letters and glanced curiously over them. Even Mr. Rhinehart, Hollings, and the others scattered to their awaiting tasks, and Christopher and McPhearson were left alone.

"That's a present worth having, isn't it?" the boy cried with delight.

"It is like a dream come true," the Scotchman answered, with misty eyes.

www.ingramcontent.com/pod-product-compliance
Lightning Source LLC
Chambersburg PA
CBHW061439210726
48287CB00007B/2278